Ann McIntosh was born in the tropics, lived in the frozen north for a number of years, and now resides in sunny central Florida with her husband. She's a proud mama to three grown children, loves tea, crafting, animals (except reptiles!), bacon and the ocean. She believes in the power of romance to heal, inspire, and provide hope in our complex world.

Also by Ann McIntosh

The Nurse's Pregnancy Miracle
The Surgeon's One Night to Forever

Cinderellas to Royal Brides collection

Surgeon Prince, Cinderella Bride

And look for the next book
Royal Doc's Secret Heir by Amy Ruttan
Available now

Discover more at millsandboon.co.uk.

SURGEON PRINCE, CINDERELLA BRIDE

ANN McINTOSH

MILLS & BOON

First published in Great Britain 2019
by Mills & Boon, an imprint of HarperCollins*Publishers*
1 London Bridge Street, London, SE1 9GF

Large Print edition 2020

© 2019 Ann McIntosh

ISBN: 978-0-263-08542-6

MIX
Paper from
responsible sources
FSC™ C007454

This book is produced from independently certified FSC™ paper to ensure responsible forest management. For more information visit www.harpercollins.co.uk/green.

Printed and bound in Great Britain
by CPI Group (UK) Ltd, Croydon, CR0 4YY

To my friend, critique partner,
and inspiration, Amy Ruttan.
Through thick and thin!

PROLOGUE

1988

IT WAS AS though Yasmine floated just ever so slightly outside her skin, so the sounds and smells of the maternity ward were muffled by the disconnect between flesh and spirit. Even the sensations of her body, the gritty pain each time she blinked her closed lids, the movement of the baby, the interminable heat, were distant things.

The observation ward wasn't full. Just her and one other lady, who was also alone. Neither of them spoke, although the curtain between their beds had been left open.

She let herself drift, leaving the agonizing present to go back in time to the night she'd lain in her husband's arms, and joy had been their only companion.

The night she'd told him she was finally, miraculously, pregnant.

Brian had been ecstatic, had shifted down in the bed so his face rested next to her belly.

"My child," he'd said. "My son or daughter. Prince or princess."

Her heart had leapt at his words.

For thirty years he'd held fast to the rule: no one must ever know who they were. What he was. Not one lax moment was to be tolerated. Yet here he was, saying it out loud. It had given her a chill, and involuntarily her gaze shifted to the closed door of their room, as though expecting people to burst through to tear them apart.

She'd had to stop herself from asking him not to say such things again, reassured herself he was using it in the North American way, as an endearment toward a child so longed for, it would be treated like royalty.

And Brian *had* longed for this child. His disappointment as the years passed and Yasmine didn't conceive was as acute as her own. Yet he never placed blame. Never suggested he should seek another woman who could give him an heir. Indeed, this baby would be heir to very little. Their need to keep a low profile had taken them to Fort McMurray, Alberta, Canada, where they'd remained.

When asked where they were from, Brian always said, "Just outside Bombay," because it was a city he'd once known well, and could make intelligent conversation about. They both had diverse ethnic backgrounds, including Indian ancestors, but in her opinion neither really looked as though they came from India. However, the Canadians they came in contact with didn't seem to notice.

Sometimes, as ethnic diversity stretched north, they got skeptical looks, but although Brian had thrown off all the trappings of royalty, he'd lost none of the confidence seemingly bred into his bones.

No one really pressed him about it.

Yasmine had simply kept her mouth shut most of the time, not completely trusting herself to maintain the fiction, should she get too close to anyone. She'd been homesick and heartsick for a lot of those years, secretly regretting not being able to go to university, having to work low-paying jobs, but having Brian made up for it all.

Now he was gone, and Yasmine couldn't find a way back into her body to mourn, or even to be angry.

Four months before, his strange symptoms had started—arm pain, moments of disorientation and lack of balance, among others. He'd made light of it all, so Yasmine had never realized the seriousness of it until he'd collapsed with a seizure at the rail yard and had been taken to the hospital. After tests and scans he'd been transferred to Edmonton, where he'd had more of both. Then the oncologist had been glaringly blunt, although Yasmine thought the sympathetic glint in his eyes somewhat negated his directness.

"It's stage four colon cancer, which has already metastasized to your liver, lungs and brain. I'm afraid there's nothing we can do, other than arrange pain management and hospice care for you going forward."

For the first time in their marriage, Yasmine had been the one to fight, to raise her voice, to insist there must be—*must be*—something they could do.

Brian had sat there, as still as the statue of his ancestor in the center of Huban, which commemorated not just the first King but also repelling the French from their shores.

The doctor had given him six months. He'd

only lived three and a half. And every moment of the time he'd had left had been devoted to thinking about their child.

"Take our child home, Yasmine," he'd said.

"To Fort McMurray? Of course." Where else had he thought she would go? At least there she knew her way around, had a job, a few friends.

"No, no," he'd whispered, squeezing her fingers. "Home, to take his or her rightful place."

She wouldn't say either yes or no. Her habitual fear may have been rendered distant and weak by the pain of watching him slip away, but it still held sway.

Finally, wanting to understand, she'd asked, "Why would you put such a burden on our child, when you didn't want it yourself?"

He'd shaken his head. "I would have carried the burden, but my need for you was far stronger than the need to fulfill my responsibilities to the country."

He had been dying by then, so she hadn't let loose the words gathering beneath her tongue, threatening to choke her if she didn't spit them out.

He'd hated it all. His unpredictable, forbidding, controlling and manipulative mother. The constant rounds of royal protocol and living in a fishbowl. When he'd told her he was taking off, it hadn't been couched as, *I can't live without you: run away with me*. No, he told her he was leaving and asked if she wished to go.

Of course, she'd said yes.

At sixteen, she would have done anything for him.

Now he was trying to push her to take their child, her baby, back to a place where, if they believed Yasmine's story, they'd take him or her away; probably imprison Yasmine too. Her father had some influence, but not enough to save her from the repercussions of that long-ago decision.

Perhaps it had been the cancer that had made Brian misremember, but Yasmine didn't have the same problem. The palace had been a frightening place; Queen Nargis a despot. She was long dead now, but Yasmine knew nothing of the family who had ascended to the throne. Father had intimated things were better, both in governance and for the people, but she wouldn't take the chance.

After all, her child would threaten their right

to rule. Who knew what they might be willing to do to hold onto power?

And when it came out that her father had known where they were, his life might be endangered too.

No. Her child would have a normal existence. As good as she and Brian…

Mind stumbling over the thought, she cupped her belly, the stab of grief like a sword inserted, twisted.

It was just her. Brian was gone.

Now her pain underwent a metamorphosis, took her to a place of clarity.

Nothing was sure. Nothing was a given.

She abruptly sat up, opening eyes closed so long the sudden light was blinding.

"Nurse." Her voice was wispy, a ribbon in a windstorm, but somehow it carried, as one of the nurses came bustling in.

"Are you in pain, Mrs. Haskell?" She immediately began checking the monitors.

"No. No. I need to see a social worker, right away."

The nurse paused, and the sympathy in her eyes was obvious. Yasmine had vaguely heard them talking through the fog of her disconnect.

"Husband died yesterday..."

"She collapsed..."

"High-risk pregnancy to begin with..."

"First child, although she's in her late forties..."

"Says there's no next of kin..."

The nurses knew she was in a bad place, and this one made no effort to offer comforting platitudes or dissuade her.

"I'll put the call in right away for you." She eased Yasmine back against the pillows, and pulled the unnecessary blanket back up over her distended stomach. "You just relax. We'll take good care of you."

Was it a premonition, or just the aftereffects of watching Brian slide away from this world to the next? Yasmine didn't know. All she could see was her baby, alone, with no one to care for him or her.

She wouldn't let that happen.

And she wouldn't let them take the baby back to Kalyana either.

CHAPTER ONE

BEYOND THE WINDOW of the hotel suite a flurry of mixed rain and ice pellets swirled, but although Dr. Farhan Alaoui gazed out through the glass, he wasn't really paying attention to the weather.

This was a fool's errand, and he the fool his father had chosen to go on it.

In years past, knowing how little regard his father had for him, Farhan would have simply refused to come to Canada, telling King Uttam to find another way to deal with the matter. It wouldn't have been the first time, or even the hundredth time, they would have butted heads. The pattern had started from when Farhan was a child, and had only stopped ten years ago, when he'd left Kalyana for Australia, cutting off contact with his father, determined not to return until absolutely necessary.

Had his conscience bitten at him over the decision? Of course it had. He'd still been mourning Ali, trying to reconcile himself to being Crown Prince in his beloved brother's place. The loss, along with his mother's unassailable grief, which had made her pull even further away from her other two sons, had been excruciating. He hadn't needed his father to intimate he was ill equipped to take on the role Ali had excelled at. Certainly hadn't needed to be left with the feeling he would never do as well, so he may as well go back to school, finish his medical studies.

There was to be a referendum, the King said, looking down his nose at his son. If they were lucky, the people would decide to make Kalyana a republic, abolishing the monarchy.

Farhan had understood what his father hadn't said outright.

If that were to happen, the island kingdom would be spared the inept and unprepared King that Farhan clearly would be.

Unfortunately for them all, the people had decided to keep the monarchy, and Farhan remained next in line to the throne. That was something he'd done his best to ignore, living in Australia as a normal person, working as a surgeon in a large hospital, until the night his younger brother Maazin had called to say their father had had a stroke.

Of course, he'd had to return then.

And he was a different person. More assured, ready to take on the responsibility he'd avoided for so long. A little less inclined to argue, or dig in his heels in the way he used to.

What he hadn't been prepared for was his father's tacit refusal to assist him in learning his new role.

Or being sent to Canada to track down the woman who should, by birthright, be the true monarch of Kalyana.

When Farhan had reported finding her, he hadn't been sure what his father's reaction would be.

Uttam's fingers had curled into a fist on his desk, and Farhan had interpreted the motion as signifying anger. Or perhaps, considering the King's unusual pallor, some other, stronger emotion. It made the physician in Farhan watch the older man closely, looking for any signs of cardio-pulmonary distress. After his father's diagnosis of atrial fibrillation the entire family worried about his health.

No one more so than Farhan.

King Uttam tapped the folder in front of him, his dark gaze boring into Farhan's. Despite the King's macular degeneration, he still had the ability to fix a person in place with just one look.

"Are you positive this woman is Bhaskar's descendant?"

Suppressing a sigh, Farhan shook his head. "I don't have Bhaskar's DNA to make the comparison. However, I can say she is a direct descendant of Queen Nargis, and since the records show Bhaskar as Nargis's only child..."

The slam of Uttam's fist on the desk was so unexpected everyone else in the office—Farhan, Maazin, and the King's aide-de-camp, Joseph Malliot—started.

"All these years our family has been blamed, accused of doing away with Bhaskar to gain the throne, while he has been out there, somewhere, living his life as he wished—"

Breaking off his unusually impassioned speech and rising abruptly, Uttam paced across the room. Stopping at the large birdcage housing his pet macaw, Uttam kept his back to his aide and two sons, reaching in to stroke a finger down Sophie's cherry-red poll.

No one spoke. Like acrid smoke, the King's words hung in the office, thickening the already tense atmosphere. Farhan sent a quick glance at Maazin. He seemed relaxed, although his eyelids were lowered, hiding his true expression.

After a moment, Uttam asked, "What do you know of her—this child of Bhaskar?"

All the information was in the file on his father's desk, but Farhan had made sure to bring his own copy.

He'd gone through it fully, of course, and memorized most of it. The private investigator had been thorough, and Farhan was of the opinion the shy and quiet doctor was not, and never would be, a threat to the kingdom.

Even her pictures gave the impression of harmlessness. She was no beauty, being a little plain, with a serious yet pleasant expression in all the photographs.

But his father wasn't interested in Farhan's opinion on things, so, opening the folder on his lap, he read out the salient facts.

"Dr. Sara Greer, general practitioner, thirty-one years old, resident of London, Ontario, Canada. She was adopted at approximately three weeks old by Karen and Everton Greer, who subsequently had two more daughters. Dr. Greer graduated summa cum laude from Eastern University, and now works at an urgent care clinic."

Uttam's free hand sliced through the air, cutting off Farhan's recitation. "Does she know she could be the rightful heir to the throne of Kalyana?"

"It would be impossible for her to know." Being on the receiving end of a quick, skeptical glare, Farhan explained, "When, as you requested, DNA was collected from Nargis's remains the results were posted privately on a number of genealogical websites. That means any matches would be reported to me, as the administrator of that DNA sample, but not to the other parties. No matter what other familial matches Dr. Greer may make, the match with Nargis is the only one that could alert her to the royal bloodline, and she can't see it."

His father's back seemed to relax fractionally, but Uttam still didn't turn around; just stood stroking the macaw's head through the bars, making Sophie chuckle and coo with pleasure.

Farhan exchanged a look with his brother, now seeing the same impatience he felt in

Maazin's expression. None of this was germane to the running of the country.

Farhan was compelled to say, "Father, this is all ancient history, and since Dr. Greer will never know who she is, she's no threat. On top of that, our constitution is clear: without documentation showing the direct lineage between her and Crown Prince Bhaskar, her claim, should she make one, would be denied.

"Adoption records retrieved by the PI show Dr. Greer's birth parents as Brian and Yasmine Haskell, residents of Fort McMurray, Canada, both deceased. Immigration records show the Haskells entering Canada in 1958 as citizens of Great Britain, although there are no records of either of their names in the British archives. Clearly Bhaskar must have had help creating a new identity, but unraveling that, at this stage, would be nigh on impossible."

He should have known better. His father was unmovable on the subject. The near rebellion caused when Uttam's father had taken the throne had, it seemed, made him paranoid. He was absolutely sure one day some supporters of the missing Bhaskar would rise up to try to end his reign, and endanger them all.

With a final scratch of Sophie's head, Uttam turned to walk back to his desk.

"We will not take the chance," he said, as he settled into his chair. "This is a matter that must be dealt with, immediately."

Despite the return of his father's usual stoic demeanor, Farhan was aware of an undercurrent beneath the cool declaration. Maazin shifted, as though suddenly uncomfortable, but before Farhan had a chance to react, Uttam continued.

"Farhan, you will travel to Canada and marry this Dr. Greer; produce an heir to unite the two lines."

Once again he felt the icy fingers of disbelief run down his spine, just as they had then.

The one thing he'd decided when Ali died was never to become a parent. His father had made it clear: the throne—the country—took precedence over everything. Farhan had no interest in producing a child only to have to sacrifice it on the altar of duty. He would do what he could to carry out the first part of his father's order, if he could, but the second part wouldn't happen.

Ever.

The door to the suite opened, rousing Farhan from his memories, and Kavan—his body-guard, chauffeur, and friend—came in, rubbing his hands together.

"How do people live in this weather all the time?" he grumbled. "It's just gone four o'clock, and it's already dark outside. Not to mention colder than normal people can bear, and the ice and slush is everywhere."

Only then did Farhan realize the murky sun-light had faded, and the street lights had come on. It was time to find and speak to Dr. Sara Greer.

His heart stuttered, but he refused to let his trepidation show. Instead he stood and walked to the hall closet to pull out his wool coat, a warm silk scarf looped under the lapels.

"There are benefits to living everywhere," he replied, as he pulled on his winter wear. "This wouldn't be my first choice, but it certainly is a beautiful country."

"In summer, perhaps," Kavan said, pulling open the room door and holding it for Farhan to precede him out. "But ice should be in a glass, with Scotch on it, not under my feet."

And Farhan found himself chuckling, despite the apprehension gnawing at his insides.

* * *

I have to get my life together.

The thought ran on a loop in Dr. Sara Greer's head as she limped from the bus stop through slush and snow toward her home.

It had been one of those days, starting from when she'd got up to find her roommate's dog, Diefenbaker, had torn the insoles out of her shoes. The right one was salvageable. The left one, not at all. And who knew there was a metal bar just above the soles? She hadn't until she'd seen it for herself. With no time to stop and buy an insole, she'd put two socks on that foot and, planning to run out at lunchtime and buy new shoes, hoped for the best.

That idea went out the window when her sister, Mariah, turned up before the clinic even opened.

"I need your car," she said, making it a demand, rather than a request. "I have an appointment at ten on the other side of town."

"Use Mom's, or Dad's." Yet, even as Sara tried to be firm, she knew it was probably a losing battle. "I have stuff I have to do at lunchtime."

"Dad's gone to Clinton to work, and Mom has some errands to run, so I need your car."

Sara's heart sank. Although her dad was a semi-retired farrier, "going to Clinton" usually meant more drinking beer than actual work, especially on a Friday during the London harness racing season. Not to mention the fact that Dad was notoriously horrible about getting people to settle their accounts. Even if he did work, he'd probably never see a dime.

And despite their perennial need for money, Mom didn't have the heart to nag him about his lack of financial acumen.

Mariah turned from demanding to wheedling. "I'll get it back to you before lunchtime. This is really important. A job interview."

"You could take the bus, you know. There's plenty of time."

"Not when I have to go home and change first. I'd need to take two buses, and it looks like it's going to rain. I'd be a mess when I get there, and it might cost me the job."

The thought of one of her sisters being gainfully employed was a heady one, given their propensity for drifting along, doing as little as possible to get by.

"Okay." Even as she capitulated, Sara knew she shouldn't. "But, seriously, I need it back before lunch. I have to get new shoes, and I promised to check in on Nonni too."

Mariah wrinkled her nose, one corner of her lip curling.

"I don't know why you bother. Aunt Jackie is there all the time with her, and she was always so mean to you. You shouldn't waste your time on her."

Sara hadn't argued the point. Mariah was right about how cruel their maternal grandmother had been to her adopted grandchild, but whatever Sara did for the now senile old woman had nothing to do with Nonni. She was helping her aunt and mother, who had given her nothing but love and acceptance her entire life.

"I promised I'd go, so make sure you bring the car back on time, okay?"

"Sure, sure," was her sister's response but, up until the time Sara's shift ended at four, she still hadn't returned it.

Then Cyndi, their younger sister, had started calling and texting at about eleven, as usual wanting Sara to intervene in one of her interminable arguments with their mother.

"She won't listen to me, Sissie." Sara knew there was nothing but trouble ahead when

Cyndi used that particular nickname. "I can't get into the culinary course on time if Mom and Dad won't pay for it now."

"I'm not getting involved, Cyndi. Sorry."

"But if you tell Mom it's a good idea, she'll listen."

Sara actually *didn't* think it a good idea for Cyndi to sign up for yet another course, when she'd failed to finish either of the other two she'd started over the last three years. Yet her saying so would only make Cyndi dig in her heels.

"Listen, why don't you save up some money and take the course the next time it's offered? That way you don't have to depend on Mom and Dad to be able to do it."

Cyndi didn't even dignify that suggestion with an answer, just moved on to the next plan of attack.

"Couldn't you lend me the money? It's only two thousand dollars."

Only? What world was Cyndi living in that two thousand dollars wasn't a lot of money?

"Firstly, I just made my student loan payment," Sara told her. "I don't have any cash to spare. Secondly, saying you want to borrow it really doesn't fly, since I don't see how you'd pay it back." Not wanting a protracted argument, she finished up with, "I have to go back to work. Talk to you later."

Undeterred, Cyndi sent so many texts, the tone increasingly desperate, that Sara had ended up turning off the ringer on her phone.

To make it all worse, the freezing cold January rain and ice mix Mariah had predicted had waited to start until Sara was standing at the bus stop. With the exception of her jacket, all the rest of her winter gear—boots, gloves and toque—was in her car. After all, she hadn't expected to have to take the bus or walk to get home.

Really, though, she shouldn't be surprised. Her family, sisters in particular, seemed to feel it was Sara's responsibility to do whatever was necessary to make their lives more comfortable, and Sara let herself be a pushover.

She remembered when Mariah had been born. Sara had already been seven when her mother had got pregnant, despite the doctors saying it would never happen, and she'd been so excited to go from lonely only to big sister. When the baby had come home, she'd eagerly helped her mother and father, and somehow it seemed she'd never stopped.

It often felt there was no time for herself, to work toward her own dreams and goals. Being viewed as an easy mark was one thing, but when you added being caught in a tug of love between Cyndi and her mom, and looking after Nonni, it often felt like too much. The emotional strain and financial pressure had stressed her to the point of a functional gastrointestinal disorder. Sometimes just seeing one of her family members' numbers pop up on her phone made her stomach roil and burn, her teeth clench.

That wasn't something she shared with her family, though. Since childhood everyone had commented on how independent and reliable she was, and, as she finally opened her front door, Sara reflected that there were far worse ways her family could think of her.

Her relief at finally getting home evaporated when, calling out to the French bulldog jumping up and down in the kitchen, she saw the note from her roommate.

Sara, going to be late. Walk Dief for me.

Not even a "please" or a "thank you."

But it wouldn't be fair to take out her bad

mood on the dog by refusing to walk him when he'd been locked up by himself all day.

"Well, Dief, since I'm already wet, we might as well go for that walk now."

And she had to giggle when, hearing her say "walk," the dog danced on his hind legs, turning in circles.

After changing into a pair of dry sneakers, Sara let him out of the kitchen and hooked his leash to his collar.

"Walkies," she sang, loving the way he pirouetted on the way back to the front door. "Walkies," she sang again, as she pulled the door open...

And walked straight into the man standing on her doorstep.

The air left her chest in a *whoosh*, and when she gasped to inflate her lungs again her head filled with the most delectable male scent she'd ever encountered. Firm fingers gripped her upper arms, steadying her as she wobbled.

Quickly stepping back and pulling a now barking Diefenbaker with her, Sara looked up.

And lost her breath all over again.

Dark yet somehow cool eyes stared down

at her from a face too pretty to be tradition-
ally handsome and yet too roughly hewn to
be beautiful. Toffee-toned skin stretched over
an undeniably masculine bone structure. Mid-
night-black hair waved back from a wide forehead, which was balanced by a strong jawline
and ever so slightly hooked nose. And his un-
smiling but deliciously shaped lips made her
legs suddenly weak.

Her heart started racing, not in fright but
with the intense sensation of recognition fir-
ing through her body, making her head spin.
Although she could swear she'd never seen him
before, something in his inscrutable gaze, the
set of his head, the scent still lingering in her
nostrils called to her primal, feminine core.

Then common sense returned.

Snapping her gaping mouth shut, she tugged
Dief close to her side. Looking down at the
dancing, yapping Frenchie gave her welcome
respite from staring at the man before her.

"Diefenbaker, enough. Sit."

Giving her a doleful glare, the little dog did
as she commanded, his barking replaced by
little rumbles in his throat.

Steeling herself, Sara looked back up and stuttered, "C-can I help you?"

Great. Not only was she a bedraggled mess, but she couldn't even speak to the most gorgeous man she'd ever seen without sounding like a dork.

"Dr. Sara Greer?"

It was only nominally a question. His deep, accented tones made it more of a haughty statement, and Sara just stopped herself from shyly dipping her chin. Instead, she forced herself to look directly into his eyes.

"Yes?"

"My name is Dr. Farhan Alaoui." He paused almost expectantly, his gaze watchful. "Crown Prince of Kalyana."

For a long moment the words sounded like gibberish. Of course she'd heard them loud and clear, but they made no sense to her on an intellectual level.

Had she fallen on the way home, hit her head and lapsed into some kind of concussed dream? That seemed more likely than a man claiming to be a crown prince standing on her doorstep.

"Wh-who?"

Obviously sensing her rising anxiety, Dief stood up and growled. Sara bent to scoop him up. The little dog was trembling—or was it her shaking that way?

"Dr. Farhan Alaoui. Crown Prince of Kalyana," he repeated, tipping his head back so he was looking down that impressive nose at her, and enunciating every syllable as though speaking to a child.

"D-don't b-be ridiculous." She could hardly catch her breath, between the pounding of her heart and rising nausea. "Is this some kind of joke? Who put you up to this?"

Her mind was spinning as she tried to figure out what was going on. There were only three people she'd shared her DNA results with, all trusted family members. Would any of them play such a cruel hoax on her?

"No joke, Dr. Greer." The corners of his lips twitched downward, reminding her of her least favorite lecturer at university. The one for whom she could do no right. "I've come to offer you a job."

"A job?" she repeated, still trying to sort

through the chaos in her head. She peeked around his broad-shouldered frame, expecting to see Cyndi or maybe Mariah behind him, holding a camera and giggling. "A-as what?"

His lips tightened, and she actually heard him inhale before he said, "My wife."

CHAPTER TWO

OF COURSE SHE thought he was crazy, although she was intrigued enough to put aside her skepticism and at least listen to what he had to say.

If even two months earlier someone had said her roots lay in the small kingdom of Kalyana, she wouldn't have had a clue where they were talking about. After getting her DNA results she'd had to look it up online.

Lying on her bed, computer on her lap, she'd fallen in love with the pictures of the country and the faces of the people. A chain of thirty-plus small islands in the Indian Ocean, it was a melting pot, she'd learned from her research. A mixture of Indian, Arab, African and European, which lent her DNA breakdown credence.

The need to understand where her ancestors came from had been growing inside her for a long time, and had become a compulsion. It wasn't anything she could discuss with her adoptive parents or younger sisters. How could she explain, although they were her family, the yearning to have a biological connection to other people, to an ancestral home, was overwhelming? Although they knew she'd looked up her birth parents' names and had done the DNA test, it wasn't something they'd talked about much, as though it wasn't that important.

Her parents had a commendable, egalitarian outlook on life.

"Everyone's the same, under their skin," was one of her mom's favorite sayings, but knowing that hadn't helped Sara when she'd been a kid, going to school, trying to field questions about her origins.

With her burnt-caramel skin tone, thick, kinky black hair, dark brown eyes and plump build, she'd stood out, especially when compared to her tall, thin, fair-skinned, blonde sisters. There had been a few other children of color in the schools she'd gone to, but the difference had been that they had all known what their roots were. Sara never had.

It had left a hole inside; empty spots in her soul.

Crown Prince Farhan seemed able to fill in

some of those blanks, although she found it difficult to comprehend what he was saying.

"Explain it to me again," she said.

Sitting in a slightly seedy coffee shop down the road from her house, she was supremely aware of the man across the table, and the avid stares of the other early evening customers. Who could blame them for being curious?

With his beautifully fitting coat, even in jeans and with a silk scarf looped informally around his throat, there was nothing casual about the overall effect Crown Prince Farhan projected.

Everything about him, from his aura of wealth to the bodyguard, who he'd introduced as Kavan, sitting at an adjacent table, was beyond Sara's, and no doubt the other patrons', ken.

It made her aware of the slightly rundown aura of her blue-collar neighborhood. Heightened her discomfort and confusion.

With exaggerated patience he replied, "In a nutshell, you're part of the Kalyanese royal family. A part that was thought to have died off."

"But I looked at my adoption records. My father was Brian Haskell, not this…"

"Bhaskar Ahuja," he helpfully supplied.

"Right. Him. So I can't be who you think I am."

"According to the DNA results, you're definitely the granddaughter of Queen Nargis, and Bhaskar was her only child. *Ergo*..."

She shook her poor befuddled head.

"This is crazy. And how does any of this relate to your proposition that we marry?"

Just saying the words made her blood pressure skyrocket, bringing a slow-building headache.

"Through your father, you could, if you wish to exercise it, have a claim to the throne. Should certain factions find that out, you may be used as a rallying point for a revolution."

"I—I don't *want* the throne," she'd said, quite sure it would be the end of the conversation. The craziness.

But Crown Prince Farhan had simply shaken his head.

Apparently, in the worlds of royalty and politics, nothing was that simple. She wouldn't even have to participate in the rebellion, could denounce it, and that still wouldn't be enough.

Farhan wrapped long, nimble fingers around

the disposable cup half-filled with coffee and leaned closer across the small table. At that distance, in the garish light, she realized his eyes weren't as dark as she'd thought.

Or as cold.

In the rich brown tones there was, she thought, a hint of sympathy, although what she interpreted as determination took precedence.

"Even though there is no way to connect Brian Haskell with Bhaskar, except through your DNA, some might consider you the true Queen of Kalyana. My father hopes that, should your lineage become public knowledge, uniting the bloodlines through our marriage would appease those inclined to overthrow his reign."

At least some semblance of her logical brain was still functioning. Not that she knew much about royalty and rights of inheritance, but she did know enough to ask, "But don't thrones pass from father to son? And if my father ran off rather than take the throne, shouldn't he be considered to have abdicated?"

He surprised her with the briefest hint of a smile. Just enough to chase the solemn, arrogant expression from his face and create deep, slashing laugh lines in his cheeks. With just that small change his face, already gorgeous, became shockingly beautiful.

Tingles of awareness shot through her veins, and heat settled low in her belly.

"Not in Kalyana. It's always been the oldest child, irrespective of gender. And there are people who might say Bhaskar was forced to run away by my family, rather than him leaving of his own accord."

A little chill ran up her spine at his words, and she had to ask, "Could there possibly be any truth to that? And if we're both part of the royal family, aren't we related?"

His face tightened, became forbidding, yet he replied, "No, we're not related and I think it doubtful my grandfather even knew he was next in line, since we'd cut off all contact with the kingdom by that point. My branch of the family had left Kalyana about a century before, and was living prosperously in Australia. By all accounts, my grandfather, his wife and children underwent great upheaval when he agreed to take the throne. And their transition was difficult, because of the suspicion surrounding your father's disappearance."

Her mind was going a million miles an hour,

and she latched onto a subject that felt distant enough to be tenable. "How old was your father when they moved there?"

His eyebrows rose slightly, as though the question caught him off-guard. "About nine or so, I think."

"Poor soul," she murmured, imagining herself at that age moving halfway across the world into a new and hostile environment. She'd had life changes happen at about the same age, and the effects still lingered, even after so many years. "That must have been rough on him."

Prince Farhan's eyes widened slightly, then he dropped his gaze to his cup, not replying.

There were too many threads to unravel, but one thing was foremost in her mind.

"Why can't I just sign a document saying I promise not to try to take over the country? Wouldn't that work as well?"

He looked up at her again, but it felt as though he'd pulled his mind back to their conversation from somewhere far away.

"The vast majority of the Kalyanese people have no problem with the monarchy. However, even after more than fifty years, the suspicions about my family have lingered, so having you aligned with our side of the family would… *should*…put all that to rest, once and for all."

It was too much to take in, and she struggled to contain her anxiety, the panic making her pre-ulcerous stomach burn and her hands shake.

Sara wasn't impulsive. She'd had neither the luxury nor the inclination to be. In life, and particularly in her job, she was cautious and deliberate, to the point where the manager of the walk-in clinic often asked her speed up diagnosing and treating patients.

And yet here she was, seriously considering his proposition.

It wasn't just the money, although the lump sum he'd offered, along with an amount he'd called a monthly stipend but had sounded like a yearly salary to her, would definitely be a godsend. More than that, though, the gorgeous man sitting across from her seemed to embody adventure, and offer her a chance to see her ancestral home. He was also dangling a chance to play a fairy-tale role in front of her like the ultimate carrot.

Her. Plain, unremarkable, sensible and reliable Sara Greer, contemplating running off into the sunset with a real life prince to become a princess in her own right?

She must be losing her mind.

As though to distract her, her brain went off at a tangent and she heard herself say, "You sound Australian, but Kalyana is in the Indian Ocean. Have your family kept their accents after all this time?"

Farhan shook his head. "I don't sound like the rest of my family because I went to medical school and practiced in Australia up until a year or so ago."

In the midst of all the nonsense, she'd forgotten he was a doctor too. Somehow knowing that made her relax fractionally.

"What is your specialty?"

"I'm a general surgeon. My brother, Maazin, is one as well, although, having trained with the Royal Guard, his experiences have been far more interesting than mine."

"Do you have a practice in Kalyana now?"

His expression was rueful as he replied, "I keep my hand in, but it feels as though I do more administrative work than actually practicing medicine. I've been trying to upgrade the medical systems, which has turned out to be more difficult than I'd imagined."

"I'd need to work, if I agree to come with you."

The words fell between them, were followed by a thick silence. Farhan's eyes narrowed, and Sara knew why.

Despite the ambivalence of the statement, it sounded like capitulation.

Hadn't she recently been thinking how much she wanted to see the place her ancestors came from? Wasn't she longing for adventure, for a chance to advance, to make things better?

I'm going to do this.

And it was, as the old saying goes, all over bar the shouting at that point.

Somehow, before going to Canada to find her, when reading the PI's report and looking at the photographs accompanying it, Farhan had felt he knew who Sara Greer was. Quiet and serious. Competent medically, but socially withdrawn. Nothing fun or fancy about her.

Yet when she'd tugged open her door before he could knock, and he'd seen her in the flesh for the first time, shock had fired through his system.

Damp and flushed, laughing down at the dog capering around her ankles, the sight had almost made him smile despite the stress he'd been under. But when their bodies had collided and she'd looked up, her gleaming brown eyes widening in shock, all his amusement had fled, replaced with a jolt of desire.

It still simmered beneath his skin, and he found himself taking in her every expression, every gesture, trying to parse them, wanting to understand what each one meant.

Not the most auspicious start to what was supposed to be strictly a business arrangement. This sudden surge of attraction was unwanted, as was the tug of sympathy he felt toward Sara Greer. Even as a child, he'd recognized the subtle danger of allowing himself to feel too much for others. Ali had been the golden son, Maazin the baby. Farhan had felt lost in the shuffle, ignored until he did something wrong. He'd craved his mother's love, his father's approval, but their attention had rarely strayed his way. Withdrawing into himself and avoiding emotional involvement had served him well.

A marriage of convenience, especially of a short duration, would suit him perfectly. With his need to serve his country foremost in his mind, he had no time for complications and messy relationships.

And it was time he made that aspect of it absolutely clear.

"What I propose is that we marry, and agree to stay together for at least a year." Something in the way her cheeks pinked up made his pulse escalate, but he kept his face expressionless, and his voice level. "Obviously, this won't be a union based on emotion and, while I'm content with that, I doubt you'd want to be locked into such an arrangement long term."

"How would a short-term marriage help the situation, though?"

"If within the year no one finds out about your lineage, I'd think it would be safe to part ways, and the chances of anyone finding out who your father was are nil. I'm sure if anyone knew Bhaskar was alive all those years, they would have said something."

The skeptical look she gave him made him impatient. She'd seemed set to agree to his terms, and now he felt victory slipping away.

"Look," he said, leaning closer over the table, trying to ignore the way the lights made her eyes seem speckled with gold dust, "I'm doing this because my father ordered me to. He's not been well, and I think he's trying to wrap up loose ends as best he can, although I suspect he'll live for many years to come. In his mind, a marriage of convenience is perfectly accept- able and you should be happy to become a part of a wealthy, royal family. He entered into such a marriage, and I knew eventually I would also, but trying to explain to him that modern women, like you, would find it strange and po- tentially insulting did no good.

"So I'm following his orders in the best way I know how, trying to be fair to you in the pro- cess. As Bhaskar's daughter you would prob- ably have inherited a bankrupt country, as my grandfather did, but I believe you're still due compensation as his heir, so think of the lump sum in that light, even though it comes with strings. The monthly stipend will be for the sheer upheaval moving and playing your part will bring."

He wouldn't tell her the deal he offered wasn't sanctioned by his father, who believed theirs would be a true, lasting union, not the limited one Farhan envisioned.

Sara still looked unsure, however, so he continued, "If after a time we part ways, my father won't be happy, but that wouldn't be his decision to make. He can order me to marry, but he can't order you to stay in the marriage if you don't want to."

"That makes sense," she said, shifting her empty cup back and forth between her hands. Then she cleared her throat, the blush now suffusing her entire face, but she bravely held his gaze as she said, "Before I agree, I have to ask: would you be expecting me to fulfill *all* the usual roles as your wife?"

He knew what she was asking; would have found her delicacy amusing if it weren't for the ramifications of even thinking that way, coupled with the rush of heat up his spine at the thought of having her in his bed.

"No," he said, quickly enough that her blush deepened. "Us being intimate isn't part of the bargain."

If his father had his way it would have been written into the contract. Uttam had gone so far as to say he would give Sara a million dollars to produce an heir within the first year, saying it might, "smooth the way to compliance." Farhan found his father's suggestion offensive in every way, and had no intention of telling her about it. Ever.

She looked back down at her cup, and he held his breath. He'd thought it would take weeks, perhaps even months to convince her to marry him, but beyond the shyness and anxiety in her gaze there was also curiosity and something akin to excitement. Farhan hoped it would be enough to get her to agree to his terms.

"Okay, but I'll need time to get everything sorted out."

Outwardly calm, but inside doing fist pumps and cartwheels, he said mildly, "That's good. You won't regret it."

Then, with ruthless efficiency, he steam-rollered over every objection that would delay their return to Kalyana, or make her change her mind as the reality of her agreement set in.

No, she didn't need time to give notice or to pack. He was royalty, and rich. They'd hire people to deal with those pesky details.

"You can leave all that to me, and we'll be on our way in two weeks."

Eyes wide, she'd gasped. "Wait. You're kidding, right?" Waving her hands, she continued, "I don't know anything about being royalty; what to do or say. It'll be a disaster, and an embarrassment. I can't do it."

"I'll arrange for you to learn whatever you need to know, as well as make sure you're completely kitted out for the part. If we get everything squared away here over the next week or so we'll go to Toronto, get married there, and then head to Paris or Milan to get you a new wardrobe."

The mingled horror and shock on her face was obvious, yet she didn't object again. Instead she muttered, "And what the heck do I tell my family?"

"The truth?" he ventured, only to be met with a scathing glance.

"Oh, heck, no. All this princess business would blow their minds."

"They'll find out sooner or later that you're marrying a prince, albeit one from a tiny kingdom."

She nibbled at the corner of her lip, and then replied, "And we're going to have to come up with a realistic backstory about how we met, and why we're marrying in such a rush."

He shrugged, and gave her a smile. "I came to Canada on business. We met and I fell head over heels for you. I refused to go home without you, and you finally gave in."

Her scathing glance and answer made him smile.

"You're going to have to come up with a better story than that. No one would believe *you'd* fall for *me* like that."

"We'll see," was all he said, rising to get another coffee, which he found to be surprisingly good. "Want another drink?"

CHAPTER THREE

FOR THE LAST month and a half Sara had lived in a fog of unreality, waiting for—no, expecting—someone to jump out of the bushes, or a doorway, or her closet, and yell, "Surprise! Got you good, didn't we?"

Even now, thousands of feet in the air aboard a luxurious private jet, and more than seven thousand miles from her home in Canada, she was quite sure it was all a crazy dream.

But the huge ruby winking from the third finger on her left hand seemed to slyly assure her it wasn't. And the still unaccustomed feeling of a horrendously expensive silk dress and amazingly comfortable, not to mention incredibly beautiful, leather shoes also hinted that what was happening wasn't an elaborate—and totally impractical—practical joke.

"We should be landing in thirty minutes, Your Highness. Can I get you anything more?"

And then there was *that*.

The title still made her want to look around to see who the other person was speaking to.

Oh, yeah. It's me.

"No, thank you, Juana," she murmured, giving the other woman a little smile.

Anything more than that tiny upward tilt of her lips was beyond her just now.

Farhan was seated at a table on the other side of the cabin with his PA, Seth Lee, official documents spread out before them. Looking over at him only made her already collywobble-infested stomach give another twist.

On the rare occasion Sara had thought of a possible husband, she'd pictured someone as ordinary looking as herself, not a man so handsome it almost made her eyes hurt just to look at him.

Even standing in front of the justice of the peace in Toronto and saying, "I do," felt like part of a dream. Farhan had tried to make it less clinical than it was in reality. The ceremony had taken place in their suite at the opulent hotel where they'd been staying, the entire living area beautifully decorated. Her cream crêpe de Chine dress had been simple but elegant, and she'd held a bouquet of vanilla orchids, their delicate petals almost the same shade as her dress but with a slightly more yellow tone. She'd learned afterwards they were the national flower of Kalyana, and Farhan, resplendent in a dark blue suit that fit his muscular form to perfection, had worn one as well, as a boutonnière.

He'd even asked if she wanted her family in attendance, but she'd declined his offer. They were already in too much of a tailspin as it was.

As though sensing her gaze, Farhan met it with his own. Cool, dark, and unfathomable, his autocratic expression only intensified her anxiety and fear. After a second, the corner of his mouth lifted in a half-smile. No doubt supposed to be reassuring, instead it washed her with heat and upped her stress quotient.

When he looked away, Sara drew in a shaky breath and turned her head, as though looking out at the clouds below.

Had it really only been just over a month since he'd entered her life, turning it upside down? It felt like much longer since her orderly, if stressful life had come crashing to a halt.

"Are you sure he isn't a sex trafficker? This is all so very sudden."

Her mother's question had made her want to laugh, but the worry lines on the older woman's face kept Sara from doing so.

"I'm sure, Mom. You can look him up online, if you don't believe me."

She'd originally planned to wait a few days after meeting Farhan to tell her parents what was happening. That decision had gone out the window when, just as they'd got back to her house, Mariah had turned up to return her car. Finally.

"And who's this?" Mariah drawled, flipping her wheat-blonde hair back over her shoulder.

"Oh, um, Mariah, meet Dr. Farhan Alaoui," Sara replied, not knowing what else to say.

"Sara's fiancé," he'd added, making Mariah's mouth drop open and her eyebrows all but disappear into her hairline.

No doubt it would have turned into a three-ring circus if Mariah's friends, waiting in another car, hadn't started calling for her to hurry up, they were going to be late.

Still speechless, Mariah had rushed off, leaving Sara to glare at Farhan.

"Wow. Thanks a lot. I better call my mom before Mariah gets to her." The weight of her decision suddenly made her shoulders drop. "I wasn't planning to tell them just yet."

His chin had tipped up in that autocratic way, and he'd replied, "I don't plan to stretch this out, Sara. So do what you have to do, as quickly as possible. We're leaving for Toronto in two weeks, at the most."

Her parents' suspicions were allayed by meeting Farhan, whom they'd invited over to dinner. Sara hadn't known what to expect. Her parents were salt-of-the-earth types, while Farhan was clearly from a whole different world.

To her surprise he'd charmed them both.

Sara had sat back, as she usually did, watching everyone interacting. Aunt Jackie had come over too and brought Nonni with her, so Sara helped the elderly lady eat her dinner, while her sisters flirted shamelessly with Farhan, until her mother put a stop to it.

"Behave yourselves, both of you," she said,

in that mild voice they all knew to take heed of. "That's Sara's fiancé you're talking to."

Only somewhat abashed, Cyndi said, "Well, do you have any brothers?"

But Farhan had just chuckled, and Dad had engaged him in conversation about horses, which had taken them through the rest of the meal.

By the time she'd left Canada, they'd had her parents' blessing, which made Sara just shake her head in disbelief. They'd totally bought her story of having met Farhan through her search for more information about her birth father, without stopping to wonder why a prince would be getting involved in something so mundane. It gave her a warm feeling, however, that none of them, not even her sisters, had seemed surprised that Farhan would want to marry her. She'd been expecting a lot more questions than any of them had seemed inclined to ask!

As though in sync with her thoughts, her phone vibrated, and she picked it up to see a message from her mother, who couldn't seem to grasp just how far away her daughter actually was.

Nonni hates the nurse you hired. Can we get someone else?

Just what she needed to have to deal with within minutes of landing in her new country. She was so nervous it took all her concentration to tap out a reply.

Sure, Mom. Just call the agency and have them send a replacement, But although Nonni has dementia she still probably realizes there's been a change and doesn't like it. You might want to give her a chance to get used to the nurse before you get someone new and start the cycle all over again.

The captain requested they prepare for landing, and Sara's racing heart dropped down into her belly as she switched off her phone before fastening her seatbelt.

Despite the coaching, the lessons in etiquette she'd diligently applied herself to over the last month, the beautiful wardrobe and jewelry, she knew she wasn't ready for this.

Was nowhere near ready to be introduced to the Kalyanese people as their new Crown Princess.

* * *

The jet taxied toward the terminal in Huban, Kalyana's capital city as the flight crew prepared for their passengers to disembark.

As he shrugged into his suit jacket, Farhan saw a sea of blue, green, and gold beyond the plane windows, as children and adults alike waved Kalyanese flags. Interspersed among them were a number of red and white Canadian flags, in honor of their new Crown Princess's country of origin.

Even from the other side of the aisle, Farhan could see Sara trembling. He felt for her, knowing how big a step she was about to take. Although she'd frequently baulked, he hadn't intended to allow her to back out, and so, with uncharacteristic arrogance, he'd simply reminded her that she'd already agreed to his terms.

Not to mention the "little" matter of their marriage, already three weeks old.

It still felt strange to think of her as his wife, although since getting to know her better he thought the arrangement, albeit not permanent, a good one. Over the time they'd spent together they'd both been busy during the day, he with official business, she with her lessons and fittings, but they'd spent their evenings together.

"It's important that we know a certain amount about each other, to make our marriage seem believable," he'd said, and although she'd muttered something about there not being much to know about her, he'd learned a lot from their talks.

Like how much her family depended on her, emotionally and otherwise.

And how much she longed to have a practice of her own, somewhere where she could build relationships with her patients, rather than have them coming in and out as if through a revolving door.

"I was born in the wrong time," she'd said one night over dinner. "Having patients I've seen from they were young, maybe even several generations of the same family, is my dream. We don't practice medicine like that much anymore."

Beneath her quiet exterior lay a compassionate heart, seemingly born to serve others. Perfect for the role of Crown Princess.

As the plane door was opened, the steps already in place outside, Farhan actually hoped he was right in that assessment, and her time in Kalyana would be a success.

He'd been aware of his interest in her growing, rather than abating, and was sure it wasn't a good thing. So he'd maintained as polite a distance as possible, and now, as he held out his hand to her, Farhan promised himself to keep that remoteness as best he could. He had no intention of making things more difficult for her, or for himself, by allowing either of them to become attached.

Sara's fingers were freezing, and trembling, and as if to negate the very decision he'd just made, Farhan rubbed them briskly between his palms.

"You'll be fine," he said. "And you look beautiful."

She cast him a grateful glance, smoothing her free hand over the skirt of her royal blue dress. Chosen by the stylist in Paris, it appeared to flow around her body, highlighting her full breasts and emphasizing her small waist in elegant, haute couture style.

Farhan found himself wondering how long it would take to unbutton all those tiny fastenings to reveal the soft skin beneath…

"Fine feathers, and all that," she muttered, yanking him out of his little fantasy. "I'll admit I'm glad your parents won't be on the tarmac. That would be truly terrifying."

Not the time to tell her Uttam terrified everyone, no matter the setting, was it?

No!

"It'll just be my brother, Maazin, representing the family, along with the parliamentarians, plus some cultural displays."

"I remember. I studied the program as though there'd be an exam on it and my medical degree was at stake."

And, to his surprise, her answer made him smile, just as they stepped to the open doorway, and cheers erupted from the crowd.

Her fingers tightened on his arm and for one moment he thought she was going to bolt back into the plane. There were foreign reporters among the local news crews, including a couple he was sure were Canadian. An official decree had gone out the week before regarding their marriage, and Maazin had told him the palace had been inundated with requests for more information. He wondered if her parents were watching back in Canada, and what they'd make of seeing their daughter this way.

Bending, he put his lips close to her ear, so as to be heard above the military band. "I think they like you already."

And, although her smile was a little wobbly, she held her head up as they descended the staircase.

Maazin waited at the bottom of the steps, a smile on his face. When Farhan had discussed with his brother their father's directive to marry Sara, Maazin had simply said, "I just hope this works out better for you than it did for me, brother."

The resignation in Maazin's voice had reminded Farhan that an arranged marriage was always on the cards, since that was his family's tradition, and three years ago, Maazin's engagement to Lady Meleena had been announced. However, only close family knew that Lady Meleena had recently left Maazin for someone else. Farhan knew he was lucky that he and Sara had entered their marriage on their own terms. There was much to be said for that.

At the foot of the stairs, Maazin smiled at

Sara. Farhan introduced them formally, and his brother bent to kiss Sara's cheeks, saying, "Welcome, sister."

"Thank you, Prince Maazin," she murmured in reply, the tremor in her voice making Maazin's smile soften in sympathy.

"Just Maazin, to you, and you're already doing wonderfully," he soothed. "Ready to run the gauntlet?"

"Wow. I was, until you called it that," she rebutted, making both Farhan and Maazin chuckle.

Sara bent to accept a bunch of flowers from a pair of children, taking a few moments to ask their names and ages, and compliment them on their clothing. The little boy and girl basked in her attention, until someone hustled them away again.

The aide charged with keeping the welcome ceremony on time started making discreet little clucking noises, and Farhan knew she wanted them to move on to the receiving line. Ignoring her, he took a moment to tuck Sara's free hand back into the crook of his arm and give her a lift of his brows.

"Shall we?"

"Yes," she replied, her voice carrying a hint of steel that made him unaccountably proud.

And his admiration for her grew as they went down the line of dignitaries. She'd obviously memorized the pronunciation of all their names and the positions they held, and, with her soft voice and obvious interest in each person, turned a formal affair into something almost intimate.

Just as they came to the end of the line, screams rang out from behind the barriers holding the spectators at bay. Farhan swung around in time to see part of the crowd surge forward, confusion threatening to turn to chaos in an instant. Police officers stationed around the runway, along with military personnel, moved to do crowd control. Seeing people falling, perhaps being trampled, caused Farhan to rush to assist, shouldering his way through the ring of palace guards that immediately surrounded them.

It was only once at the barrier he realized Sara was right behind him. Before he could stop her, she slipped beneath the arm of a soldier trying to hold back the panicked crowd and disappeared into the swirling mass of humanity.

"Sara!"

Heart thundering, he shoved past a police officer to plunge in after her, just as the small stampede petered out.

Sara was kneeling, hunched over a woman who was lying on the ground curled into a ball. She had her arms curved protectively around the woman's head and, as Farhan strode toward them, he heard the distinctive screams of a young child.

A member of the Royal Guard got to them first and bent to say something to Sara, who looked up and waved him away.

"I need to examine them, see what their injuries are," Farhan heard her say, as he got to her side. "No, I won't leave you to take care of them."

"Stand down, Major," he said.

"Yes, Your Highness." The soldier saluted and stepped back, and if Farhan hadn't been so angry at the fright she'd given him, he might have found the sympathetic glance the soldier gave him amusing.

Before he could say anything, Sara snapped,

"Get an ambulance. She has a laceration on her arm, and I don't know if she or the baby have other injuries."

His training took over, and as the major spoke into his headset, summoning medics, Farhan shifted to the opposite side of the woman.

"Lie still," Sara said to the young woman, who, after starting to roll over, froze, then stared up at Sara and Farhan, her mouth agape in shock. "Let me take a look at your baby."

With a bit more coaxing, the woman let Sara take the baby and set him across her lap, where she could inspect him more carefully, while Farhan began his visual examination of the woman.

"Where hurts?" he asked, but the woman only blinked, making no attempt to answer.

He took her pulse, found it strong and only slightly elevated. But when she tugged her wrist free, he made no attempt to do anything further. Some of the women from more traditional backgrounds were uncomfortable with having a male doctor and, realizing she may be one, he decided to wait for the medics.

One of his first acts since coming back to Kalyana had been to revamp the emergency system, recruiting more women paramedics for just such a situation. It had been a fight, but he'd got it done.

"It's okay, little man," Sara was cooing to the little boy, her nimble, sure hands examining the squirming infant.

As though hypnotized by her attention, the baby quieted, and by the time the medics ran up he was smiling up at her, arms and legs waving freely.

Something shifted in Farhan's chest to see Sara cradling the baby in her arms, warmth flowing out to settle in his belly and climb his spine. It was a picture of tenderness, as close to motherly love as it could be without it being her own child.

Why that had him staring, his insides churning with a sensation he didn't recognize and didn't wish to put a name to, he didn't know.

She looked up then, their gazes colliding. Her eyes gleamed softly, and her lips were curved into a sweet, gentle smile.

Then the smile faded from her face and a touch of color stained her cheeks as she quickly looked away, turning her attention to the medics and relinquishing her hold on the infant.

As two female paramedics fitted the mother with a cervical collar, Farhan rose to get out of their way and held out his hand to help Sara to her feet. Her previously neat coif was a little disheveled and, along with her rosy blush, brought to mind that first startling moment he'd seen her, realized her quiet beauty.

"Your Highnesses." The protocol aide, followed by Sara's new assistant, Mara, came rushing over, and were let through the cordon of soldiers surrounding them. Farhan tore his gaze away from Sara to give the aide his attention. "You're behind schedule now, and Princess Sara will have to freshen up before the audience at the palace."

"Oh, but the children haven't had a chance to sing for us yet. They'll be terribly disappointed, having waited in the sun for so long." Sara turned questioning eyes to Farhan. "Can't we at least let them do one song before we leave?"

No, they couldn't. They were due at the palace at a specific time, and it wouldn't do to keep his father waiting.

Yet he wavered, unaccountably wanting to make her happy.

Maazin came over, brushing off his uniform, having also jumped into the fray.

"It was a bench that collapsed under the weight of people standing on it. The injured are being taken to the hospital. We should be going. Is there a hold-up?"

And Farhan heard himself say stiffly, "My wife would like to hear the children sing." He turned to the aide and said, "Please advise the palace there will be a small delay."

He turned away to offer Sara his arm, but not quickly enough to miss Maazin's raised eyebrows and grin.

Dammit, it was her first day in Kalyana, and if she wanted to hear the children sing, then let her hear them sing!

CHAPTER FOUR

EVEN WITH THE DELAY, they got to the palace on time, and with Sara buffed and polished. With ruthless efficiency Farhan arranged for Mara to travel with them in the limousine, and her personal assistant efficiently brushed a smear of dust from Sara's dress, as well as fixing her hair and make-up.

Not that Sara made the job easy for her.

"Please, Your Highness, if you could turn your head this way…"

But Sara could hardly take her eyes off the people lining the streets, the scenery visible beyond the colorful buildings.

Kalyana was gorgeous, and seeing it, and its people, made her heart sing.

She'd never felt more excited in her life.

It truly felt like coming home.

Perhaps not the smartest way to feel, since she was only here for a relatively short time, but it was impossible to ignore the way her heart pounded with joy.

The royal palace was on a hill, and her first glimpse of it made Sara gasp. It was like something out of a fairy-tale. Not a European tale, though, something more Eastern.

She'd seen pictures of Moorish castles, and Huban Palace seemed closer in design to those.

The walls of warm-hued stone gave a sense of solidity, but the ranks of arched windows lightened the fortress-like façade. Ringed by lush vegetation and bright flowers, it was a picture-perfect scene.

And the interior of the palace was so gorgeous she stood for a moment, gaping like the country bumpkin she knew herself to be.

They walked through huge, wonderfully carved doors into a majestic entranceway of creamy stone walls, with two curved staircases sweeping upward on either side. Intricate carving adorned the arches around doorways and gave life to the stone balustrades, while the marble floor gleamed beneath their feet, reflecting the colors of massive floral arrangements.

Her awe only intensified when she was presented to her new father-in-law.

At first Farhan's resemblance to his father made her want to smile, but King Uttam's steely scrutiny made her nape prickle with discomfort.

"Princess Sara." His voice matched his cool gaze, increasing her nerves.

"Your Majesty," she murmured, as she curtsied the way Mara had taught her, feeling slightly silly as she did so. Sara secretly thought all the pomp rather pointless. Nevertheless, despite the transient nature of her involvement, she wouldn't embarrass Farhan by not following protocol.

Well, unless it involved watching the school children, dressed in tropical colors, faces bright with pride and excitement, sing a traditional folk song. Then protocol and schedules could go hang.

The Queen gave Sara a small smile, but had little to say beyond welcoming her, and Sara noticed the sadness in her eyes. It was so very similar to what she'd noticed in Maazin's and she wondered if it had anything to do with the death of Crown Prince Ali and his wife, ten

years before. When she'd read about the trag-
edy in the book she'd been given to familiar-
ize herself with the country's history, there'd
been little detail. She'd wanted to ask Farhan
what exactly had happened, but it seemed too
intimate a subject to bring up.

Now, even more than before, her curiosity
was piqued.

Thankfully, the King and Queen didn't seem
inclined to get to know her better, and they only
exchanged small talk regarding their trip and
the welcome ceremony. There was to be a family dinner later, but she breathed a sigh of relief when Farhan escorted her from the throne
room after less than an hour.

With the long flight from Dubai and the excitement of the day her neck muscles were aching and her body felt heavier than usual.

Yet, when Farhan suggested she might want
to rest for a couple of hours before she had to
dress for dinner, she found herself saying, "Actually, I'd like to go to the hospital and check
up on the people who were hurt this afternoon."

"That isn't necessary, you know. There are
perfectly competent doctors to look after them."

She shrugged lightly. "I'm sure there are,

but I feel somewhat responsible. I just want to know how everyone is doing."

The glance he gave her made butterflies start fluttering in her stomach, and she was reminded of the moment they'd shared at the airport, when he'd looked at her in a way he never had before. When her heart had leapt, heat creeping through her veins to warm her through and through.

Thankfully, this time his gaze didn't linger on hers. Instead he turned back to look where he was walking.

"We can certainly do that, if you wish, but it might cause a bit of a commotion. You are, after all, royalty now, not just a doctor popping in to check on her patients."

"Don't remind me," she muttered.

He chuckled. "It gets easier, believe me."

As he summoned a car for them, and after she'd refused his offer for her to change, since he wasn't going to, Sara went back over the events of the day.

Farhan had been angry with her for running to help the young woman earlier. She'd seen it in his eyes. But there was something else bothering her, and she was in two minds about whether to tax him with it or not.

Then she got distracted by the fact it was an SUV that was brought to a side door for them, and that Farhan, rather than a chauffeur, was going to drive it.

"No Kavan to drive you?" she asked, since the other man had hardly seemed to leave Farhan's side while they'd been in Canada and Paris.

"When I'm here in Huban I usually drive myself, and don't feel as though I need a bodyguard. I sometimes take him with me when I visit the other islands, but more for convenience than out of necessity. He has a pilot's license, so he can fly if I want him to, and if I'm tired after a long day at a clinic, it's often nice not to have to think about navigating narrow, winding roads."

There was something reassuringly normal about getting into the passenger seat, having him get behind the wheel.

And that sense of normality made her relax for the first time that day, and gave her the courage to ask, "Earlier, I noticed you didn't try to examine the baby's mother. Was there a reason for that?"

She was almost fearful of what he might say, since she couldn't think of any good reason why he wouldn't have done so, but there were a number of what she would consider bad ones.

"Some of our more conservative residents don't look kindly at their female family members being touched by males outside their family, even a prince. When I took her pulse, she pulled her arm away, so I didn't want to make it uncomfortable for her, and didn't try to do anything further."

Her relief was sharp, and a bit ridiculous. Why should she care whether he was a snob or not? She already knew he was arrogant, didn't she? His being elitist shouldn't make any difference, but it would have.

"Ah, that makes sense, and explains the two female paramedics." Rolling her head against the headrest so as to look at his profile, she asked, "Have you set up a women's clinic yet? Somewhere the women can go, knowing for sure they will see a female doctor?"

As they were saluted through a gate, Farhan brought the SUV to a stop to check for oncoming traffic, then made the turn before he replied.

"It's on my list of recommendations, which I suspect is gathering dust on the Minister of Health's desk, or perhaps has already found its way into the dustbin."

That surprised her. "But you're the Crown Prince. Shouldn't they be doing what you say?"

Farhan chuckled, but there was little amusement in the sound. "I was gone for a long time and, since coming back, have been made completely aware of how little influence I really have. It was a fight just to get more female paramedics trained. Perhaps if I'd been here over the last ten years it might be different but, as it is, I have to pick my battles."

Sympathy wasn't something she'd ever expected to feel for her arrogant husband, but it moved through her now.

"That must be incredibly frustrating for you. And, now that I think about it, would you have to set up a series of such clinics, for the various islands? I didn't really consider the logistics of it."

He nodded. "For administrative purposes the islands are clustered into eight districts, each district having as few as one island or as many as five. My recommendation was to start with two clinics, one here in Huban and the other in the Southeast District, which is the next most populous, to serve as many women as possible."

"That makes sense," she replied, distracted by the various sights they were passing.

Beyond the windows was a combination of newer buildings and older, some colonial in style and others simple wooden structures. The city glowed like a jewel in the bright afternoon sun and, with the cerulean sea visible in the distance, it all made Sara's heart lift and soar with pleasure.

In Canada the winter winds were howling still, snow or slush and ice on the ground, everyone bundled up against the cold. Here in the southern hemisphere it was summer, and she knew from her research that the temperature wouldn't get much lower even in the winter season.

It felt so right. She'd always disliked winter. Oh, she was used to it, and fully equipped to get through it, but she'd had to monitor her moods to ensure she didn't fall into depression, and use a daylight lamp to get the Vitamin D her body demanded.

"It's so beautiful," she murmured.

"Some of the other islands are even more so," he replied, as they turned into the hospital grounds. "We'll have to make arrangements for you to see some, if not all of them."

There was no more time to talk as they drew up beneath a portico, and she saw two women in somewhat old-fashioned nurses' uniforms and a man in scrubs standing outside turn to stare.

"Don't be surprised at the fuss that's about to ensue," he warned, as he opened his door, but there was a teasing tone to the remark, so Sara didn't pay him too much mind.

She should have though, as their arrival created excitement far beyond what she'd expected.

"Y-Your Highnesses," the young man outside the front door stammered. "I don't think anyone told the director you'd be coming, or he'd be here to greet you."

"That's fine, since he didn't know. The Crown Princess wanted to check on the people hurt this afternoon," Farhan replied.

He looked as stern as usual, and both the doctor and nurses looked terrified, so Sara tried to defuse the situation by smiling at them and saying, "This isn't an official visit, just a spur-of-the-moment thing. There's no need to disturb the director."

"He'd be very displeased, Your Highness, if no one informed him. May I suggest coming with me to his office, or giving me the opportunity to call up and let him know you're here?"

Silently sighing to herself at the proposed delay, which would no doubt mean *not* seeing what she wanted to, Sara replied, "Of course you must tell him if you think that's best."

Farhan interjected, "Dr...?"

"Patel, Your Highness. Imran Patel."

"It's a pleasure to meet you, Dr. Patel. You must have been exceptionally busy whenever I've been here in the past for us not to have crossed paths before."

The young doctor's eyes blinked rapidly a few times before he replied, "I'm still very new here, sir. Doing a residency under Dr. Anwar."

"Ah, one of our finest internists." He turned to Sara, and she couldn't help noticing the twinkle in his eyes. He was up to something. "My dear, we should find Dr. Andrade, the director, so we don't get Dr. Patel into trouble. While he and I do that, I'm sure these ladies will be happy to show you to the wards where the patients are."

She couldn't help smiling back at him in appreciation. Their time was limited, and he knew she didn't want to waste it with nonsense.

"That's a wonderful idea." When she turned to the nurses, she only just stopped her smile turning into a grin at their expressions of mingled amazement and pride. "As long as it won't be any trouble. I know how busy you nurses always are."

"Oh, no, Your Highness. No trouble at all," the older of the two replied, while the younger one's face glowed with a blush.

Before any of them could change their minds, Sara headed into the hospital, the nurses a step behind.

But, even with Farhan's warning, she found it difficult to understand the upheaval that took place wherever she went in the hospital. People bowed, often with palms together, fingers pointing upward, some of the women curtsied, and work stopped as people stared at her going past. Many of the staff and patients seemed too tongue-tied to answer her questions, so she checked charts and said encouraging things to the injured, letting them know she hoped they recovered soon.

It was tiring, and made the quick check-in she'd wanted take far longer than she'd expected. She'd been glad, but also disappointed, to hear the young mother and baby she'd helped at the airport had already been discharged. While she was happy neither had been seriously hurt, she'd also hoped to get one more chance to hold the baby.

She also noted that while the hospital wasn't as modern as those she was used to, with some of the wards open to the outer air and the layouts somewhat inefficient, it was scrupulously clean, and the equipment was up to date.

As they were leaving the last patient on the women's ward, she heard a low moan from behind a curtained bed, and stopped, arrested by the utter agony of it.

"That's not one of the patients from the airport, Your Highness," Kadiah, her nurse and guide, said quickly.

Too quickly, Sara thought.

Ignoring Kadiah's apparent hope she wouldn't investigate, Sara stepped across and slipped between the curtains.

There was a woman lying on the bed, curled into a ball, holding her abdomen. Perspiration dotted her face, and her lips were dry and cracked, but it was the low, rhythmic groaning that made the hair on the back of Sara's neck stand up.

Touching the patient's face told Sara her temperature was elevated, as was her pulse when she checked it. Stepping to the foot of the bed, she picked up the chart stored there and quickly scanned the information. What she read made her blood boil.

She turned to the younger nurse.

"Deena, please go and find Prince Farhan. Ask him to come here, immediately."

CHAPTER FIVE

THE TWO NURSES froze for a moment, but before Sara could reiterate her command, Kadiah nodded at Deena, and the younger woman took off, speed-walking out of the ward.

"Why hasn't this woman been taken to surgery already?" Sara could hardly contain the anger in her voice. "It shows here that Dr. Patel diagnosed her with a ruptured appendix and abscess over three hours ago, and she's been ill for over a week. If she's not operated on as soon as possible she could develop sepsis, if she hasn't already."

Kadiah explained, "Dr. Patel has been trying to contact the surgeon on call, Your Highness, but hasn't had a response."

"But Prince Farhan is here now. Dr. Patel should have informed him of the problem and asked for his help."

"Yes, Your Highness, but we were specifically told not to bother the Crown Prince while he was on his honeymoon."

Taking a deep breath, Sara tamped down her emotions, consciously relaxing her grip on the clipboard in her hand. It was no use arguing about it now. The patient was all-important.

"He'll need an operating room, surgical nurses, and an anesthesiologist. Can you arrange that, please? As quickly as possible."

"Yes, Ma'am."

She too rushed from the room, leaving Sara with the patient, whose name, according to the chart, was Eshaal Saleem. Anger still shimmered under her skin, but she acknowledged the unfairness of blaming either Dr. Patel or the nurses. They had been doing as they were told.

Blowing out a calming breath, she slotted the chart back into its holder and looked around for something positive to do while she waited.

There was a bowl of water beside the bed, a washcloth submerged in it. Fishing out the cloth, she wrung it out and leaned over to wipe the woman's face.

"You'll be all right, Eshaal," she murmured, hoping she was pronouncing her name correctly. "We'll take good care of you."

The woman's eyelids fluttered then lifted for a moment, before wearily closing again.

As she ministered as best she could to the patient, Sara was suddenly struck with a disturbing thought.

She had no way to know how Farhan would react to being volunteered to operate. It wasn't something she'd given a moment's thought to. In her eyes, it was the right thing to do.

But would he feel the same way?

Dread swamped her, making her hands tremble as she wrung out the cloth again. Despite earlier reveling in the heat, now the sultry air suddenly seemed so oppressive she could hardly catch her breath. When brisk footsteps heralded Farhan's arrival, nausea threatened, and Sara swallowed thickly against it, afraid of revealing her weakness in front of strangers.

In front of him.

"Sara, you wanted to see me?"

Why did he have to sound so grim, so terrifying, most of the time?

Gathering all her courage, she turned to face him and, hoping he wouldn't notice the sheen of perspiration on her forehead, lifted her chin.

"Yes. I think you should examine this patient."

Farhan's expression didn't change, but his gaze sharpened. Without taking his eyes off Sara, he stepped farther into the cubicle to pick up Eshaal's chart.

"Oh?"

He looked down to read the notations and Sara almost gasped with the relief of being released from the hold of those deep, inscrutable eyes. Taking a deep breath, she decided to go all in.

"I've asked for an anesthesiologist to be called and an operating room be prepared for you, since they've been unable to contact the surgeon on call."

"Oh, that won't be necessary." Sara had been so focused on Farhan she hadn't paid any attention to the other man, who she now assumed was the director, Dr. Andrade. "I'm sure the on-call surgeon will be found soon enough, Your Highness."

"Will he?" Farhan asked, his deep voice quiet but with what sounded like a dangerous tone to Sara. "It says here that Dr. Patel made these notes three hours ago. Is that accurate, Dr. Patel?"

Poor Dr. Patel looked from Farhan to Dr. Andrade and back again, his Adam's apple bobbing convulsively a few times, before he answered, "Yes, Your Highness."

"And there's been no response from the surgeon?"

Farhan had replaced the chart and moved to Eshaal's bedside, beginning his examination.

"No, sir."

Kadiah slipped back into the cubicle and Sara raised her eyebrows, sending her a questioning look. The nurse nodded in reply.

Farhan spoke gently to the pain-racked woman as he palpated her stomach. Then he straightened.

"Has Mrs. Saleem signed the consent form?"

"Yes, sir," Dr. Patel replied. "And her husband is waiting outside to hear from the surgeon too."

"As soon as the anesthesiologist arrives and is ready, I'll operate. Does anyone know when he or she'll be here?"

Kadiah spoke up. "Dr. Tam is on call, sir, and Dr. Patel had already put her on notice that she'd be needed, so she'll be here in about ten minutes."

"Thank you. I just need to make a phone call and speak to my wife, then I'll go and scrub in."

Sara's heart raced, her anxiety ratcheting up a notch. All she could hope was that he wasn't too upset, and wouldn't tear a strip off her where anyone could hear. She didn't think he would. More likely he'd be cold and cutting, but that would be just as bad.

"You can use my office, Sir."

Dr. Andrade made the offer but Farhan, who had already taken out his cellphone, just shook his head.

"Thank you, but I think the verandah will be fine. Sara?"

She preceded him back through the ward to the open doors leading to the wraparound balcony. There was one corner, near a set of stairs, that seemed to offer a bit of privacy, so she made a beeline there.

If she was going to get a talking-to, she wanted as few people as possible to overhear.

Farhan was saying into the phone, "Kavan, sorry to bother you so soon after you got home, but could you pick up Princess Sara at the hospital and take her back to the palace? Thank you... I'll let her know."

As he touched the screen to hang up, he said in a distant tone, "Kavan will be here to pick you up in about twenty minutes."

"Okay," she muttered, braced for whatever would come next.

Farhan's eyebrows dipped together. "What's wrong?"

Might as well get it out in the open, and take whatever he had to say on the chin.

"I'm sorry for putting you on the spot like that. I didn't think it through. It's just that she's going to die if nothing gets done soon."

The words were rushed, and little more than a strained whisper through a throat tight with stress. Farhan's frown deepened, and her heart sank. Putting her hands behind her back, she clasped her fingers together and squeezed, hard, using the pain to center herself.

Farhan's expression lightened, and he shook his head. "I was angry with you earlier when you rushed into the stampede, and I'm upset with the surgeon who's missing in action. I'm even annoyed that no one told me about this patient sooner, but I'm definitely not angry with you. You did the right thing."

Relief arced through her, making her scalp tingle and her legs wobbly. Why it was so strong, she didn't know, but she was forced to turn away so he couldn't see the moisture gathering in her eyes.

She heard his footsteps approaching, but wasn't prepared for the weight of his arm across her shoulders, or the safety and contentment the gesture immediately brought. When he bent his head and placed his lips close to her ear, Sara stiffened, not with surprise but in an effort to suppress the shiver creeping up her spine.

"I know we don't know each other as well as we could, but never doubt that my first responsibility is to the people of Kalyana. It is my duty to do all I can for them, and that includes using my medical training."

His arm tightened around her shoulders for an instant, and goosebumps fired along her arms and up her torso.

"If anything," he continued softly, "I should apologize to you."

"Wh-what for?"

"For leaving you to face my family alone

this evening. There's no way I'll get finished in Theatre in time for dinner, but thank goodness it's not formal, just my parents, Maazin, and some close family friends."

It was daunting, just the type of situation that should send her anxiety levels through the roof and have her ulcer burning, and yet...

"Your parents are a little scary, especially your father, but somehow I'm not too worried."

"Really?"

The touch of humor in his voice made her smile.

"Maybe because of our arrangement, I know it doesn't really matter whether your parents like or approve of me or not," she replied, recognizing the truth in that statement.

And wondering why, then, *Farhan's* approval meant so much!

King Uttam had a favorite phrase.

Punctuality is imperative.

He was also known to elaborate on this philosophy.

"If you are five minutes early, you are already ten minutes late."

The King didn't make those statements lightly.

In fact, each of his sons had, at one time or another, been on the receiving end of a lecture, or gone without supper, for being tardy.

In the palace the standing rule was: if you are not going to be on time, do not turn up at all, as you will not be welcome.

Normally Farhan adhered to that rule, because although he was no longer the young, awestruck boy who feared his father, it was just simpler. As an adult he recognized his mother's discomfiture when his father made cutting remarks and the atmosphere turned cold, and tried to spare her when he could.

So on the few occasions he had to miss a family gathering because he was in the operating room, Farhan stayed away.

Tonight, however, was different.

Sara deserved his attendance, even though she'd assured him she'd be fine.

Even if his late arrival had the potential to make King Uttam apoplectic.

Having showered and changed into dinner clothes, Farhan strode into the dining room, a determined smile on his face.

The assembled group was already having dessert, and silence fell, as though no one could believe his temerity. Cheerfully he greeted his parents, their friends, and Maazin, before walking directly to Sara. He bent and kissed her cheek, and she stiffened slightly, although she didn't pull away. Probably he should've made the salutation brief, but he instead let his mouth linger for a moment longer than necessary, enjoying the soft warmth beneath his lips.

"How did the operation go?" she murmured.

"It went well. She has a long road ahead, but I'm assured she'll recover fully."

The smile she gave him more than made up for his father's glower.

"I'm afraid you're too late for dinner, Farhan." There was no doubt about the annoyance and command in his father's voice.

"That's fine, Father. They kindly fed me at the hospital. I would, however, love some of that trifle."

For a second he thought his father was going to tell him it would not be allowed, but when the King merely frowned before taking another bite of his own dessert, the butler hurried to bring a serving of trifle for Farhan.

"Are you sure you've had enough to eat?

There must be some lamb left, if you're still hungry," said Sara.

Not a surprised silence now, but one of shock at her egregious breach of protocol—although Farhan doubted Sara noticed. She was completely focused on *him*, the concern in her dark eyes filling him with joy and the kind of tenderness he'd never thought himself capable of. There was a spluttering sound from Maazin's direction—probably a stifled laugh—but Farhan couldn't tear his gaze from Sara's. Tingling warmth spread through his belly and up his spine.

"Anyone who is late to my table does not get fed."

His father's cold words thankfully broke the spell. Sara blinked, then turned her attention to the King. Farhan expected her to blush, or stammer, the way she did when he spoke to her, but, instead, she just smiled faintly.

"And no doubt that discipline was instrumental in your sons becoming the men they are now. I wish my parents had been stricter with us, for just that reason."

Farhan snapped his head around so fast to see his father's reaction it was surprising he didn't get whiplash. Yet what was truly shocking was watching Uttam's lips twitch at the corners.

"Perhaps the first time I've ever heard a child say such a thing about their parents." Looking down at his trifle, the King continued. "Farhan, Maazin, I suggest that you listen carefully to everything Sara says from now on. She's obviously extremely intelligent and may even be a good influence on you."

They all stared at him, Farhan wondering who this man smiling down into his pudding was, and where his father had disappeared to.

Then his mother giggled, the sound so unexpected, so sweet Farhan found himself joining in. Sara lost it next, with Maazin and his parents' guests following right after, until the entire dining room rang with laughter.

It was like being in a dream, surreal. Especially when he looked at his father and found him still smiling into his beard.

Uttam had never been particularly congenial, and what vestige of humor he'd once possessed had seemed to have died with Ali.

To see him like this was a revelation…

And a relief.

Somehow the woman sitting across from him,

her face glowing with humor, had already made a huge change in all their lives.

Especially his.

Now all he had to figure out was why she exerted such a pull on him, and how he could resist.

CHAPTER SIX

DINNER WAS A lot less stressful than she'd expected, but Sara knew part of that was her own attitude toward the entire royalty issue.

Frankly she couldn't give a hoot about whether they could trace their lineage back a thousand years, or that they ruled an entire—albeit small—country. If her parents had successfully taught her anything, it was that everyone deserved the same respect.

That attitude was coming in mighty handy just about now. But although she was fine with treating King Uttam as though he were her elderly next-door neighbor, and Maazin like a brother, she couldn't get over her hyper-awareness of Farhan.

From the moment he'd walked in her calm had all but deserted her, leaving instead a tingle dancing just under her skin. Knowing he was putting on a show for the others when he kissed her cheek didn't stop her heart from jumping, or her traitorous body from wanting to melt at his feet.

Telling herself it was just because he was so incredibly handsome didn't help, or even ring true. While they were different in appearance, some people would say Maazin was even more attractive than Farhan, but Sara's pulse didn't race when she saw him. Electricity didn't spark through her system, neither did sexual tension tighten her nerves.

No, Maazin did nothing for her in that regard, whereas Farhan made her think thoughts so naughty she was sure her cheeks were constantly aflame whenever he was around.

She'd never had anyone affect her that way before, and she wasn't sure how to handle it. Ignoring it would probably be the best thing, but there was no way to stop her visceral reaction to his scent, his nearness, his dark, often mysterious gaze.

Even now, hours later, she could easily recall the sensation of those gorgeous lips on her cheek and the memory made her nipples tighten, warmth filling her belly.

Thankfully, when they cited their long day and said goodnight to the older couples, leaving them to their after-dinner cocktails, Maazin excused himself too.

"I'll walk with you," he said, as they exited the sitting room, not into the corridor but onto the verandah outside.

"Going out this evening?" Farhan asked.

Maazin gave him a strange look, one that Sara couldn't decipher.

"No, I have some paperwork to finish up. I thought I'd go back to my office and get it done."

"All work and no play..."

Maazin just shook his head and bent to kiss Sara's cheeks.

"Goodnight, little sister, and most annoying older brother."

"What was that all about?" Sara asked, as Maazin strode off toward the east wing, where she supposed his office was located.

Farhan didn't answer immediately, just took her hand and tucked it into the crook of his arm, to lead her along the softly lit walkway.

Thinking he wasn't going to answer, she tried to ignore the heat of arousal building in her body by looking out over the extensive parklands stretching away from the palace. Beautifully landscaped, they sloped down into a small valley and gleamed softly in the light of the waxing, gibbous moon rising beyond the distant hills. A lovely floral aroma wafted on the warm breeze, but it wasn't enough to mask Farhan's masculine scent, which went straight to Sara's head like a shot of rum.

"Maazin has no social life, hasn't had one for years. He's a workaholic, getting old before his time, trying to make up for something I, personally, believe he should forgive himself for."

"What did he do?" Perhaps now she'd learn what that sadness was she saw in Maazin's gaze when he thought no one was looking.

Farhan moved her hand from his elbow and, instead, entwined his fingers with hers, linking them in a way that intensified the intimacy of their conversation.

"He was a hell raiser when he was young, and fell in with a bad crowd. One night he went to a party out in the countryside, got drunk and fell asleep. When he woke up, his friends had left him. He walked far enough to get cell signal and called our brother, Ali, asking him to come and get him. I think he knew if he called one of the guards, or anyone else, they'd tell

Father what had happened, but Ali always looked out for us."

She knew what was coming, wished she didn't have to hear it.

"They got into an accident on the way home. Ali and his wife, Chandni, who'd gone with him, were killed instantly, while Maazin only had a badly dislocated shoulder."

"I'm so sorry, Farhan."

He squeezed her fingers. "Don't feel badly. It was a long time ago, and it's time Maazin got past it."

Yet, even with his factual recitation and acknowledgement of Maazin's pain, she knew his brother wasn't the only one still adversely affected. She'd only just met them, but she was sure it explained so much she'd already noticed. The way the family interacted, as though each inhabited a bubble the others could see through but never penetrate.

"Easier said than done, I should think. The same for the rest of you too. You were away when it happened?"

Now he stopped to rest his back against the balustrade, turning her so she stood in front of him, their fingers still linked. Though he made no move to urge her closer, Sara wanted to lean into him, the magnetic pull she always felt suddenly overwhelmingly strong.

His face was partially shadowed, but his gaze still easily snagged and held hers.

"I was in med school, in Sydney. I came back as soon as I could, expecting to have to stay and take up where Ali left off, even though I was already working toward my fellowship."

There was a sense of having to tread gently, but he had brought it up, so she asked the obvious.

"Why didn't you stay?"

His lips thinned for an instant, then he replied, "My father said it wasn't necessary; told me to go and complete my surgical training."

It had hurt him. She didn't know how she knew, but she was sure of it.

"You all must have been grieving so horribly then. Shock and pain make people say things, make decisions they might not have otherwise." Here in the moonlight, it was easy to open up to him. "When my grandpa died, my mother's family pretty much imploded for a while."

His gaze was searching.

"What happened? Was your *nonni* heartbroken?"

The sound she instinctively made was derisive, and she regretted it as soon as it came out. She'd tried to make peace with her feelings for Nonni, but obviously she hadn't succeeded.

"No, although she was the source of the rifts that opened up. You see, she'd run off and left Grandpa and her three children something like twenty years before. No one knew where she was in all that time, until she turned up one day at Aunt Jackie's, asking if she could stay with her to recover from a bad motorcycle accident. Aunt Jackie didn't know what to do. She didn't want to be disloyal to Grandpa but, being the youngest—she was only six when Nonni took off—she wasn't as angry, I guess, as Mom or my Uncle Ed.

"Plus, Aunt Jackie's marriage had just ended. It was a bad time for her, and she ended up taking Nonni in, after getting Grandpa's blessing. About six months later, Grandpa had a massive heart attack, a widow-maker, and that's when things fell apart."

She could still remember it, as though it had happened the day before. Uncle Ed shouting that Aunt Jackie had broken Grandpa's heart by taking Nonni in; Nonni making things worse by not staying out of it.

"What happened?"

Sara shook her head, trying to push the memories back.

"My uncle blamed Nonni and Aunt Jackie for Grandpa's death, and said he was done with the family. Never wanted to see any of us again."

Farhan squeezed her fingers.

"How old were you?"

"Eight, almost nine." She inhaled, then let the air out in a rush. "It was pretty traumatic, to be honest. There was a lot of dirty laundry aired, and a lot of mean things said. For about a year Mom didn't speak to Nonni or Aunt Jackie either, and it took Uncle Ed five, maybe six years to speak to either of his siblings again."

"Did your grandmother at least try to smooth things over?"

"That isn't her way, or wasn't before she developed dementia. She was the type of person who said whatever she wanted, and damn the consequences. I think she enjoyed making people angry. At least I'm sure that wasn't your father's intention when he said what he said to you."

Farhan's lips firmed into a hard line, but then they relaxed again into a sad smile.

"Ali was…special. The perfect son. The best of brothers. I think, when Father told me to go back, I used it as an excuse to not try to fill Ali's shoes, because I knew I couldn't. Not in a million years. Staying away was easy after that."

But why hadn't his father asked him to come back or, as she suspected would be more King Uttam's way, commanded him? Sara suspected Farhan thought it was because, in King Uttam's eyes too, he wasn't worthy to take his brother's place.

"I'm sure Ali was special, but you have so much to offer Kalyana too. Maybe what you bring to the table is different, but don't sell yourself short."

Farhan didn't reply, just stared at her for a long moment. The air between them seemed infused with electricity, so the fine hairs on Sara's arms lifted, and, although she felt suddenly shy, she couldn't look away.

Then he turned his head, as though looking

out over the gardens, and when he looked back at her, her breath hitched in her throat, although she didn't know why.

Swinging her hand back and forth, he asked, "I meant to ask you earlier: are you comfortable with our suite? There are many others we could move to, if you aren't."

She shook her head, surprised at the sudden change in topic. "You're kidding, right? It's beautiful."

And it was, although to call it a suite was damning it with faint praise. It was like a house within the palace, complete with a central courtyard where a fountain played the soothing sounds of splashing water. Huge rooms, decorated in keeping with the rest of the palace, had creamy marble floors offset by lush carpets and intricate decorative painting on the walls. Touches of turquoise, gold, and red turned the living area into a feast for the eyes, and her bedroom had literally taken her breath away when she'd first seen it.

All white and gold, with fuchsia accents, it was the most feminine yet restful room she'd ever seen. The bed was a huge four-poster, draped with sheer panels, while gold-framed mirrors lined one wall.

She still hadn't gotten over the bathroom, with its mosaic tiles and sunken tub either.

Farhan lifted one shoulder, in an abbreviated shrug.

"That one is old-fashioned. It hasn't been updated in decades. There are others more modern, if you'd prefer."

"No. Seriously, I love it. Please, can we stay there?"

He chuckled, reaching out to smooth a little curl of hair off her cheek, and replied, "Of course."

When had she moved so close to him? The thought had hardly entered her mind when he gently tugged her closer yet. Near enough that the heat of his body touched her like a caressing hand, and his mouthwatering scent completely filled her head.

Part of her wanted to step forward and experience the thrill of his muscular body against hers, but the saner part of her had her stiffening, stepping back. She could only go so far, however, since he was still holding her hand.

"You have to get used to my touching you."

There was no amusement in his voice, just a deep, velvety tone that made her legs tremble and heat flow out from her core.

"I—I don't see w-why."

Good grief. She hadn't stammered since she'd been in fourth grade, but whenever Farhan got too close her tongue refused to co-operate.

"We're married, Sara. If we're to make people believe it's true, you can't pull away every time I touch you."

"I—I d-don't!"

His free hand came up to skim her arm, a gentle, evocative brush of fingers, his thumb finding the ultra-sensitive inner flesh. An intense flash of yearning raked her, and she jerked.

"See?"

"You startled me."

How absurd to be proud of not stammering, of holding up her head when she wanted to duck and hide.

"Come here. Let me startle you a little more."

She should resist, not let herself be drawn in, physically and figuratively. Her experience with men was limited.

Okay, pretty much non-existent. One abbreviated love affair in med school, which had ended when the guy decided she spent too much time and energy on her family, hadn't prepared her for Farhan Alaoui.

There was no way she could tangle with him and not get severely emotionally injured, especially knowing this was all a ruse to him. A joke played on his father, and the world.

Yet, when he gently tugged, she went to him, the motion as natural as breathing, swallowing.

Living.

His arms went around her, not too tightly, just enough to bring their bodies into soft alignment, and she forgot how to breath or swallow.

But, oh, she was instantly, completely, fully alive for the first time.

His hard frame shouldn't be so comfortable or his grip evoke such safety, even as arousal swirled through her, tangling up her common sense, blurring her reasoning capabilities. How had she never known a hug could be so glorious, leave her desire-struck, melting inside, even as every sense sharpened almost painfully, so she could soak in his every nuance?

"Did I tell you how beautiful you look tonight?"

That had her stiffening again, need draining away, leaving her bereft and damp-eyed, wanting to step back but not wanting him to see her silly tears.

"Don't, please."

But he wasn't so easily dissuaded.

"Don't, what? Tell you how lovely you look? Why not?"

There were no easy answers to his questions, only prevarications or self-pitying proclamations about long ago having accepted her own plainness. If she was honest, she would stay right where she was for as long as possible, and listen to him lie about her beauty as much as he wanted.

Yet she was a pragmatist. There had never been a time when she'd been able to avoid or evade reality, and this wasn't a good time to start. But she stayed where she was, taking the crumbs of intimacy he offered, too weak to pull away.

Hiding as best she could, even as she stated the brutal truth.

"I don't need you to tell me things like that, Farhan. I know I'm no beauty, and even these gorgeous clothes can't turn a sow's ear into a silk purse."

The sound he made was one she didn't recognize, and she didn't expect his arms to pull her closer yet, bringing her flush against him, from their hips to their torsos.

"Oh!"

"Yes," he murmured, bending so the word whispered over her ear, making her shiver, a little moan rising in her throat. "Does that reassure you I'm not lying?"

Did it?

Sara had no brain power left to work it out, not with his erection resting against her belly, his breath rushing hard against her cheek, one hand sliding over her back, the other coming up to cup the back of her head.

He kissed her cheek, but there was nothing casual or cursory about the movement. It was, instead, as though he tasted her, explored each millimeter as he went, his lips seemingly learning things about her she somehow divined on a cellular level.

Like how to arouse her, to fill her with mindless lust, so that when his mouth reached hers, she was ready to accept whatever he had to offer.

Fingers thrust into her hair, he tilted her head back and paused, their lips only a breath apart.

"Sara." There was a question in her name, and she wasn't sure what he was asking, her cognitive abilities impaired by his nearness. Her need. "Sara, may I kiss you?"

How could those words make her want him even more than she already did?

"Yes."

It whispered from her lips onto his, acceptance and surrender all in one.

He kissed her slowly, gently, his lips brushing hers, coaxing, playing. She lost track of time, forgot her fears about her inexperience, instinct guiding her to open to him, to taste him as he tasted her.

Farhan groaned, deepening the kiss. They were fused together, her fingers clutching the back of his jacket, desperately seeking an anchor in a world gone haywire beneath her feet. Those same fingers longed to know what his sleek, hot skin felt like, just as the rest of her body yearned to find out too.

When his lips left hers to travel down to her

throat, she could hardly stand, her entire body trembling, aching for him.

"You're delicious."

The words rumbled into her flesh, and a rushed sound of assent rose in her throat, blocking it, rendering her unable to reply.

Her head dipped of its own accord, giving him complete access, and he took full advantage of her compliance. With lips and tongue and teeth, he brought every nerve ending to sparking, shivering life.

A sound came from below, the echo of footsteps, the quiet drone of conversation. Sara hardly registered it, but Farhan slowly raised his head, a sigh whispering between them.

The sudden distance between their bodies came as a surprise, and it was only Farhan's hands on her shoulders that stopped her from swaying, perhaps even falling.

"That went further than I planned." His voice was cool, and she wondered how he went from the heat of passion to his usual icy self so swiftly, when she could still hardly catch her breath. "But don't worry. It won't happen again."

How to respond to that, when everything inside her wanted more of his kisses?

Luckily, she didn't have to reply as he continued, "I like you, and now you know I'm physically attracted to you, but our situation could get…messy if we aren't careful."

Not sure what he meant, she repeated, "Messy?"

His chin tilted up in that way it so often did. "Yes, as all relationships do when there is emotion involved."

Ah. He was afraid she'd fall for him and get silly. Knowing that steadied her, and gave her a jolt of moxie too. She replied in as light a tone as she could manage, "I wouldn't worry too much about that. I can't speak for you, but I've no interest in getting emotionally entangled. With all I go through with my family, I have enough of that in my life as it is."

Farhan nodded slowly, and offered her his arm as he turned toward their suite. "I should have known you were too sensible not to understand."

All Sara could do was walk alongside him,

willing her still trembling legs not to let her down and wondering why hearing herself described that way annoyed her the way it did.

CHAPTER SEVEN

THE FOLLOWING FEW days were a whirlwind of activity, and Farhan watched Sara manage it all with commendable aplomb.

The day after their dinner with his parents, he'd gone to the hospital to check on his patient first thing in the morning, and then there was an official reception in the palace gardens, followed far too swiftly by a state dinner.

"Your wife is making quite an impression on everyone," Maazin commented to him at the garden party. "She's very charming, in her quiet, easy way. Just as you are, when you aren't playing Crown Prince."

Ignoring his brother's jab, Farhan replied, "She's a born giver. I'll have to make sure no one takes advantage of her."

"Well," Maazin said, laughter in his voice, "Glaring at the people she's speaking to will definitely do the trick."

Realizing he probably did look rather fierce,

Farhan forced himself to adopt a neutral expression just as Sara glanced back and gave him a smile. Something inside him softened, and he couldn't help smiling back.

The night before she'd taken his statement about not wanting to get tangled up in emotion well, yet now he wondered if he weren't the one who needed the warning. The taste and feel of her were indelibly locked into his memory, and he wanted more of both. But the danger of forging emotional ties with her wasn't something he wanted to contemplate.

Yet later, seeing Sara in the soft pink sari-inspired ball gown she'd donned for the dinner, which hugged her luscious curves in all the right ways, was another revelation. It made him want to turn her around and take her somewhere private, not share her with the world.

It was, he reassured himself, just physical attraction. All his energy had to be channeled into his position, the work he was trying to do for his country. Sara would be gone in a short time, but Kalyana would continue on, and he had to be prepared to lead her into the future.

On Sunday, they were expected to attend church in the cathedral and afterwards had another round of official visits and introductions. As he explained to Sara, it was better to get it all over with as soon as possible, rather than stretch it out over a couple of weeks.

"If we did that, I'd get no work done at all."

"That makes complete sense, especially since I'm looking forward to going back to the hospital and seeing what I can do to help out."

She'd seemed understanding, but he'd also seen the fatigue in her eyes, and the way she locked her fingers together when she thought no one was watching. Hopefully being back in a medical setting would alleviate some of her stress.

He knew he should be as aloof as possible with her, yet her warmth and genuine personality made him also not want to hurt her in any way. There was no mistaking how she fractionally withdrew each time he forced himself to be cool with her and, strangely, it hurt him too.

Yet it also reinforced the knowledge of his own shortcomings, the part of his character so reminiscent of his father. The ability to pull away from people, to lock away his emotions, become cold and clinical. She deserved better, even in a pretend husband, but Farhan wasn't prepared to open himself up to the danger of caring too much for her, only to have to send her away.

On the other hand, Sara was, in some ways, irresistible. Okay, in many ways. If they were separated during official functions, he found himself in her orbit, keeping an eye on her, moving closer and closer, until he was back by her side.

And when she smiled at him in seeming relief, the sensation of being her champion filled him with warmth.

And desire.

Desire she seemed to share.

Walking back to their apartments, she said, "It's so interesting meeting all these people, hearing their stories. Everyone I've spoken to seems very happy to have you back in the country and so engaged."

Her words shouldn't please him so much, but they did. However, he was cautious in his reply. "I doubt anyone would tell you otherwise, Sara. After all, you're my wife."

Her hand on his arm stopped him in mid-step,

and when he turned to face her, the earnest expression on her face was arresting.

"Farhan, as a doctor, don't you know when your patients are skirting the truth? Like when you ask how much they drink, or smoke, and they give you an answer, but just from their demeanor you know it's probably more?"

"Yes." It was indeed something he'd learned to watch for.

"Well, it's something I'm very good at, and I can usually tell when someone's telling the truth or just schmoozing. You have nothing to worry about when it comes to whether you're appreciated here or not."

There was such sincerity in her voice, her soft gaze, he found himself stepping closer, his heart unusually light. Lighter than it had been in a very long time. Perhaps since the night he'd heard of his brother's death.

"Your Highness," he murmured, teasing in his tone. "If you're not careful, you'll turn my head, saying things like that."

And his heart raced when she blushed.

Irresistible, in all ways.

Leaning against the wall, so she knew she

could step away if she wanted to, he eased her warm body into his arms.

She didn't pull away but wrapped her arms around his neck, although she murmured, "Farhan, someone might see."

Sliding his lips close to her ear, he whispered, "See me kissing my wife? I think that's acceptable."

"In the hallway?" Her question came out in a rush, her voice breathy, hopefully from the sensation of his teeth gently playing with her earlobe.

He searched for her lips, halted with his a millimeter away from her sweet, seductive mouth.

"We're the Crown Prince and Princess. We can kiss wherever we like."

Then he put action to his words, tasting and sipping until she opened for him, their kisses getting deeper and deeper, until he knew he had to stop, lest he drown. Seeing her flushed, her eyes gleaming, lips damp, was almost his undoing. It took him close to forgetting his finer instincts, his need close to pain.

Drawing away, putting a stop to it, was far more difficult than he liked, and turning the conversation back to safe, boring topics took everything he had. But it had to be done, for his own safety and sanity.

On Monday, he came out of his bedroom after another restless night where his dreams were bedeviled with images of Sara, to find her already up, dressed and ready to go.

"You're going to the hospital this morning, right?"

"Yes," he replied, sitting at the breakfast table and smiling his thanks to the young woman pouring his coffee.

"Good. I'm coming with you. There's no way I'm sitting around here all day with nothing to do."

Even if he wanted to gainsay her, the smile lighting her face when he nodded would have changed his mind.

As soon as she entered the hospital there was a flurry of excitement, which she quelled with a few calm, well-chosen words.

"I'm here to work, not disrupt anything. Take me up to the director's office and let's figure out where best I can help."

That was the last he saw of her, except for glimpses of her hurrying off down corridors, totally unaware of him staring after her, wondering why the hospital, which had been a refuge for him, now felt like a jail.

Then his father called, catching Farhan in his office just before he went in to operate on a young man with a diaphragmatic hernia, and demanded their presence at dinner.

Clearly Farhan wasn't the only person fascinated with Sara. In the year since he'd been home, they'd established a routine of family dinners once every two weeks. Of course, he saw his parents at other times, and his brother almost every day, but to be summoned again so soon made Farhan wonder what his father was up to.

Ali's wife had been the child of a wealthy Indian businessman who was one of Uttam's oldest friends, and the match had been conceived between the fathers and dutifully carried out by the children. She'd been used to a far grander, more cosmopolitan life than Kalyana could offer, but Ali had been devoted to his position, determined to assure his father the throne would be in safe hands after his death. Chandni had accepted that, and had set out to make a place for herself in Kalyana, although she had never been as hands-on as Sara seemed determined to be.

Queen Aruna had loved Chandni, and she and her daughter-in-law had taken trips together to Dubai, Milan, Paris, and London to shop and enjoy the bright lights. His mother had been devastated by the loss of Ali and Chandni. She'd never been the same. An air of sadness enveloped her even ten years later, and she'd become reclusive, the world outside the palace seemingly holding no interest for her anymore.

Sara wasn't like Ali's wife, who'd been worldly and supremely elegant, and Farhan hoped she didn't suffer by any comparisons.

As he'd suffered from being compared to Ali.

Before going to surgery, he went looking for Sara to tell her about his father's invitation, or command, depending on how one chose to look at it. He found her in the clinical area, where non-emergency patients came for treatment.

"You're lucky this wasn't worse, but because of how it happened, I'll be prescribing antibiotics. Are you allergic to any medications?"

Even over the hubbub of the clinic, his ears picked up her soft, calm voice immediately, and he drifted toward the cubicle it was coming from.

"No, Your Highness."

The curtains weren't pulled closed, so he peeped in, glimpsing Sara stitching a gash on an elderly woman's leg. Then he stepped back so as not to be noticed, leaning on the wall across from the cubicle to wait for her to finish.

"Will your son or daughter-in-law be able to help you for a few days? You should stay off this leg as much as possible to give it a chance to heal. And I want you to come back and get the bandages changed for at least three days, so we can make sure it's healing properly and there's no infection."

As he listened to her instruct the patient, interjecting little comments that made the elderly lady laugh, he was struck by the way she connected so easily with the other woman. It was apparent she'd learned a lot about the patient's situation in their time together, not just a medical history and information about her immediate ailment. Farhan liked to think he had a pleasant bedside manner, but now he wondered if it was as sorely lacking as he was beginning to think.

Realizing Sara was finishing up with her patient, he moved over to the nurses' desk, so neither of the women exiting the cubicle would realize he'd been eavesdropping.

They both saw him as Sara helped the limping lady toward the waiting area, and the elderly patient whispered something to Sara that had her blushing and saying, "Hush, you!"

Her patient laughed, and paused to greet Farhan in traditional Kalyanese fashion, her palms together, head bowed.

Before he could offer his assistance, a younger woman came hurrying over and, with much bowing and thanks, the patient was helped on her way.

Sara stripped off her gloves and tossed them into the nearest medical waste receptacle.

"Took a fishhook to the thigh, poor soul. And she's diabetic, too."

It seemed she'd been avoiding looking at him, but suddenly faced him head on, a frown between her brows. "I gave her a prescription for antibiotics. Do you think she'll be able to fill it? I can see she's not terribly wealthy. Is there another way I should have handled that?"

Totally unprofessional to want to hug her in the middle of the clinic, but that's exactly the urge Farhan had to fight.

"No," he replied, shoving his hands into his pockets so they wouldn't embarrass him and grab her. "It should be fine. The government has a subsidy program in place for medications and if she can't pay the rest, there are other programs for that too. I think you'll find the patients who can't afford it will say so, because often they can get the drugs free here in the hospital dispensary before they go, and they want the voucher immediately."

The palpable relief on her face made a flash of warmth fire along his spine, and he quickly told her about his father's invitation, and high-tailed it back to his office.

Putting thoughts of anything other than his patient out of his mind was imperative before going into the operating theatre, but it wasn't as easy as usual. His wife had a very unsettling effect on him. One he knew had to be curbed, for both their sakes.

Scrubbing in, he went over the upcoming surgery in his head. The patient lived on a small island forty-five minutes away from the capital, accessible by private boat or public ferry. Unfortunately he'd ignored his symptoms for a while, thinking he had a gastrointestinal ailment, but after four days of vomiting and beginning to have trouble breathing, he'd gone to the local clinic. X-rays had shown an anomaly in the left thoracic cavity, and the doctor had told him to make the crossing to the hospital in Huban.

Subsequent tests had revealed the presence of a Bochdalek hernia, strange in that those were usually congenital and the patient couldn't recall any trauma he'd suffered to explain its sudden development.

Farhan was glad, however, that it appeared, at this point, repairable by laparoscopic surgery. Of course, if once he got a look inside there was a sign that any of the displaced organs were gangrenous, they would have to open the patient up. Then what was normally a ninety-minute operation would be much longer.

As the nurse put on his gloves, Farhan found his mind drifting once more to Sara. The blush that had bloomed in her cheeks when the patient had whispered to her had him wondering what had been said.

"Your Highness, they're ready for you in the OR."

The nurse's quizzical tone brought him back to the moment, forced him to put it all from his mind as he shouldered his way through the swinging doors.

Perhaps his fascination would fade if they spent even more time together? Farhan couldn't decide if that would be the best or worst thing ever.

"Your Highnesses will make beautiful babies."
While busy in the clinic, Sara tried to put her patient's words out of her head but they lingered.

Farhan had made it clear there would be no intimacy between them, yet twice now he'd kissed her senseless. Mind you, immediately afterward, while she'd been trying to figure out up from down, he'd reverted to his usual autocratic self as though nothing had happened.

His blowing hot and cold was so confusing.

And Mrs. Ramakesh's comment had made

her wonder something she'd not given any thought to before.

Wasn't one of Farhan's duties to produce an heir? Thinking about it, there was no doubt in her mind that Uttam was demanding one.

Was that why Farhan kept initiating intimate moments between them? Was the entire population of Kalyana watching and speculating about when she'd become pregnant?

His assertion about them having to be comfortable with each other to make their marriage seem real had made sense at the time, but now she questioned his motives.

And his kisses hadn't made her more comfortable. If anything, her awareness of him, already intense, had been heightened. She'd tossed and turned for the last few nights, reliving each moment, every touch of his hands, lips, tongue. Just thinking of it now made her temperature rise and tingling, needy warmth trail through her body.

As a doctor, she knew her physiological reactions were normal. After all, there was nothing wrong with her libido; no trauma in her past to give her a psychological fear of sex. Yet it had never been terribly important to her either.

She'd been too darned busy studying, working, and trying to keep her family afloat to give it much headspace. The one relationship she'd thought might lead to intimacy had died on the vine, a casualty of her complicated life, and she'd put that aspect of life on hold.

And it might have stayed that way until she'd opened her front door and seen Farhan standing on the other side.

Now desire infiltrated any brain cell not otherwise occupied, which seemed to be far too many of them. Work usually completely consumed her, but although she was fully engaged in the jobs at hand, doing whatever came her way with customary care, Farhan was constantly on her mind.

And what had been the expression on his face earlier, when he'd told her about his father's invitation to dinner? One moment he'd seemed pleasant, approachable, the next closed off, looking down that arrogant nose at her. It was horribly confusing, and just one more reason not to trust that his kisses stemmed only from attraction.

Confrontation wasn't in her comfort zone when it came to personal matters, but by the end of the day she realized that speaking to Farhan about the matter of an heir was imperative. For her own peace of mind, if nothing else.

So, on the drive home, while they were alone, she took a deep breath and said, "I get the feeling we're under scrutiny, everyone watching to see if I get pregnant. I hope that wasn't part of your plan in marrying me."

The look he slanted her from the driver's seat was so autocratic it almost made her courage flee.

"It was not." There was no mistaking the steel in his voice. "I have no plans to procreate with you, or anyone else."

Shocked, she turned in the seat so as to better see his face. "Why not? Well, I know why not with me, but why not with anyone else, after our marriage is over?"

"Being ruler of Kalyana is a full-time, twenty-four-seven job. Fatherhood would have to take a backseat, and I don't think that's fair to a child."

His cool, controlled tone didn't fool her. Behind it was a shadow of pain, of rejection, and her heart ached for him. For the little boy, the young man she could somehow picture. The one who'd needed his father in a way the older man had been unable to fulfill.

She'd come to know Farhan, at least a little, over the time they'd spent together and couldn't, somehow, bear the thought of him going through life depriving himself of something she was positive he would excel at.

Carefully, trying to tread lightly, she replied, "Perhaps your reign will be different, because you're different from your father. I think you could be both an excellent father and King at the same time."

Farhan shrugged slightly, his eyes firmly on the road ahead. "My father is a good ruler, well respected and effective. I'd like to be the same."

"I have no doubt you will be, when the time comes, but what happens if you fall in love and the woman wants children?"

"Love doesn't come into the equation. I'm not even sure I'm capable of it, since I've never felt it, or sought it out. It's never been a part of my plan, since arranged marriages are traditional in my family. Once Ali died, I knew one day I'd enter into one, and since I couldn't offer a real relationship, I made sure not to lead women on."

He'd shielded his heart, she thought, rather than risk having it broken by falling for someone and then having to let them go. Still intent on his profile, she contemplated the loneliness he must have felt, both as a youngster who'd just wanted his father, and as a man who didn't dare to love. She'd often felt an outsider, alone because of not knowing where, exactly, she came from. Now she realized that having the deepest of roots didn't make everything magically better. In fact, it could isolate you from the world even more.

She ached for him, wished she knew the right words to make him see how amazing he was, and make him believe it.

His eyes met hers, caught her staring. Trapped, she froze, her heart suddenly hammering. Then he looked back at the road, and she gazed down at her fingers, knotted in her lap, able to catch her breath again, although the air in the SUV felt thick.

Then Farhan broke the silence. "I've decided to push really hard on the idea of women's clinics across the kingdom, but I'm going to need your help."

Surprised, she glanced back up at him. "My help? In what way?"

He made the turn into the palace grounds, raising his hand to the soldier at the gate before he replied.

"I'm going to arrange a tour of the islands for us. We, you in particular, can speak to the women and get their input on what's actually needed. What they say will hopefully make it harder for the minister to keep putting it on the back burner."

That sounded innocuous enough. "You know I'll help however I can."

"Good," he replied, in that stern way he had of speaking.

Why, then, did her heart jump and her body tingle in anticipation?

CHAPTER EIGHT

THEIR PLAN, ACCORDING to Farhan, was to take three weeks or so, going from island to island, working their way from north to south. What she hadn't really considered was that they would be going alone, since usually they were constantly surrounded by people.

Yet here they were, just the two of them in an amphibious plane, heading to the northernmost island, Agung.

No Kavan.

Or Maazin.

Or even assistants Mara and Seth.

Just her and the man whose mere presence made her want to jump out of her skin. Whose large, capable hands were controlling the plane with ease and assurance, reminding her of how masterfully they'd held her.

It was still so confusing, though. He'd kissed her so passionately, yet otherwise kept a respectable distance, keeping her on edge, waiting, wanting to be intimate that way with him again. The memories of his kisses kept her awake at night, need a constant tingle in her veins, shaken to her soul with desire.

Worse was imagining what else they could do together, how it would feel to be skin to skin with Farhan, having her every need met.

"We'll be there in just under an hour."

His voice came through the headset she was wearing, the warm, rich tone raising goosebumps along her arms.

"Okay."

He seemed different once they got to the airport. More relaxed. Perhaps it was just being able to get out of the capital for a while, or out of his father's sphere.

King Uttam had commanded their appearance at dinner twice more during the preceding couple of weeks, and there was no mistaking the chill between the two men. Father and son had a distant way of interacting and Sara now had an idea of why, even as she realized where Farhan had inherited his arrogance.

Yet seeing him in that light didn't ring true to her anymore. What she'd ascribed to bone-deep haughtiness was overshadowed now by what she'd seen since they'd come to Kalyana. The way he spoke to his patients and the staff at the hospital, his interactions while doing his royal duties all spoke of a man deeply connected to and concerned about others.

If anything, seeing him that way made her want him more. How many times had she caught herself staring at his mouth, entranced and aroused? Thinking about it now had heat gathering in her belly, rising up to her cheeks, and she turned to look out over the azure water below so he wouldn't see her blush.

Over the last few days she'd found herself wondering if Farhan might not be the perfect man to gain some sexual experience with. After all, their temporary marriage was without all of the emotional baggage that could make a physical relationship messy, and at least now she knew he wasn't trying to seduce her in hopes of producing an heir.

On top of which, she had no intention of falling for him, and after their talk had no fear he'd fall for her either. If he truly was interested in sleeping with her, why not give in to her own desire?

Her brain shied away from the thought, too

exhausted to process it properly. Besides not sleeping well, it felt as though they were constantly on the go. Not that she minded working at the hospital. That, at least, brought some normality to her life. Practicing medicine was what she was born to do, and it made her happy to help people. But all the other stuff? Trying to remember the correct protocols, watching every word coming out of her mouth, every gesture she made? All that did was tire her out and give her tension headaches.

Not to mention the constant barrage of texts from Canada, none asking how she was doing but all wanting her to help or advise in some way. There was no let-up.

Farhan had told her she was doing well, but she knew she'd made some missteps. Caught between wanting to be herself and not embarrass Farhan, the strain was immense.

"Look over there," he said, pointing to the east, the motion of his hand wafting his compelling scent her way. "That's Patang, or Kite Island. It's not much more than a sand bar, but because of the reef on the western side it's a great place to swim, and on the east, if the conditions are right, you can surf."

"Why's it called Kite Island?" she asked, twisting slightly in her seat to get a better view. The water surrounding the part of the island she could see was a shade of aqua so intense it looked as though it had been enhanced digitally.

"It's roughly diamond-shaped, with the reef coming off one end like the tail of a kite. When we come back I'll fly closer, so you can see. Actually, since we're not really on a tight agenda, we could go there."

"If you like," she replied, too tired to really care.

"It was one of our favorite places to go as children. Ali loved it, especially when the waves were high and he could surf. Believe it or not, my father was a good surfer too, and even my mother enjoyed a day at the beach."

Her ears pricked up. Here was a memory that seemed to belie his sense of his father having no time for his family. It was the first time he'd spoken of him in such a fond, reminiscent way.

"I can't imagine your father surfing."

He chuckled, then replied, "I'm not surprised, but remember, he grew up in Australia and was already surfing by the time he moved here."

She still couldn't picture it. "I can't even think of your father ever being a child, much less a surfer dude."

Farhan laughed. Not a chuckle but a full-on laugh. It was such a rare thing she wanted to watch him at it, but forced herself not to look. Except she could still see his reflection in the glass beside her, and realized she was already fixated on that.

"So he was more approachable when you were young?"

Amusement dropped from his face, and she regretted its fading as he replied, "Approachable isn't a word I'd ever use to describe my father, but he was a bit more...mellow...before my grandfather died and he took the throne."

"Perhaps he was patterning what he'd seen as a child. From what you said and I've read, your grandfather inherited a mess when Nargis died. He was probably consumed with trying to put the country to rights, without a lot of time to spare."

For a few moments the hum of the engines was the only sound in the cockpit, as Farhan fiddled with the controls.

Finally, he said, "That much is true. The

country's finances were in a shambles, mostly because Nargis wouldn't stop spending money. She was a compulsive collector. Not to mention what she spent trying to find out what had happened to Bhaskar. My grandfather had to rebuild the economy in the face of staunch opposition from those who'd benefited from Nargis's rule. They didn't like it that he was trying to create a more egalitarian society."

"Were you close to your grandfather?" From her calculations, Farhan would have been about ten when his grandfather had died.

"Not really. He loved horses and playing polo, and I didn't, so we didn't have much in common. Ali was the one who was into those things."

Another male figure who'd shown Farhan little interest. No wonder he thought taking the throne would mean giving his children short shrift. She wasn't going to point that out, though, but maybe she could give him something to think about. Plant a seed in the hope it would flower into something good after she was gone.

Why did the thought of leaving make such a wave of sadness flood her?

Pushing her own feelings aside, she said, "Well, your grandfather and father had the worst of it, I think. Barring disaster, you're inheriting a far more stable country, in pretty good financial shape, thanks to them."

"That is true." Farhan sounded distant, almost disinterested. "And sound economic management isn't a trait many of the rulers before them had."

He seemed to want to turn the conversation away from the personal, and she followed his lead.

"Oh, but the royal family has had some hard knocks too, haven't they, over the years? Like the plane crash that killed five members. That must have been a horrible blow."

The look he gave her warmed her from head to toes, and all points in between, although she wasn't sure why.

"That's right. That happened just after the start of World War II. You really dove into the history of Kalyana, didn't you?"

"I—I have almost perfect recall of things I read." Why was she stuttering? God, she was so silly sometimes. "And it was interesting, trying to figure out how your family ended up inheriting the throne."

"Yes. The plane crash in 1940, then the war. The tradition of younger sons going into the army took its toll, with three Princes being killed between the two World Wars. Then there were a couple of Kings who didn't or couldn't procreate. By the time it got down to Nargis, the line of succession went to Bhaskar, and then to her sole surviving uncle. When Bhaskar disappeared, the uncle was already on his death bed, and the next in line, as crazy as it sounds, was my grandfather."

Sara sighed, thinking about what he'd said, that ache she'd carried in her heart all her life intensifying. "It must be nice to know your history that way, know exactly where you come from and how you ended up where you are."

The touch of his fingers on hers was a warm surprise and, unthinking, she turned her hand, linking them together.

"It's your history too, beautiful. You've found your place, your family's past to add to your own."

Something opened inside her, pain cracked wide by his words. She looked over at him.

Farhan was smiling at her, his eyes warm and understanding.

Welcoming.

What he'd said was real and true, something she'd never thought, even after the DNA test, finding out about her biological father, or reading the history of the Kalyanese royal family. Until he'd said those words she'd been the perpetual outsider looking in. But now...

"Thank you," she whispered.

His eyes darkened, his smile faded. Sara's heart lurched, then raced, as his fingers tightened on hers, and dangerous sparks seemed to fill the air between them.

Then he turned back to the controls, letting go of her hand.

Trying to catch her breath, she looked down at her lap and her empty hand.

"Was it difficult for you, growing up as an adopted child?"

He asked it casually, as though giving her a chance to tell him to mind his own business. Funnily enough, she had no qualms about answering, even though it was a subject she usually avoided.

"For the most part, no," she replied. "You

met my parents. They're great people and even when Mom had Mariah and Cyndi, they never treated me as anything other than their child. Most of the rest of the family was the same."

"Most?"

The sharpness of his tone made her look his way, but his expression was bland, and now she hesitated to answer. It was a subject she never spoke about, even with her family.

Then she reminded herself it was a long time ago, ancient history, and she should be over it by now. Besides, for some unknown reason, she wanted to tell him.

"When Nonni came back into our lives, it wasn't easy. She said some pretty hurtful things about me, and they mostly kept me away from her after that. It was scary, at that age, to feel as though someone hated me that much."

"What kinds of things did she say?"

There was no mistaking the dangerous tone in his voice, and somehow it lightened Sara's heart, taking the sting out of the well-remembered words.

"Oh, that my parents had no idea where I came from, and I could be the child of a murderer. And that no doubt I'd turn out to be a thief and, once I'd taken everything I could from them, would run off, leaving them destitute."

"Good God. And you were how old?" The horror in his voice was like a balm to her soul.

"Eight, almost nine. I think that's why, when you mentioned the age your father was when they moved here, surrounded by suspicion and tension, I could relate."

Farhan was silent for a moment, his face tight, and the look he sent her was filled with a mixture of anger and sympathy.

"That explains a lot," he said, rather cryptically. Then, before she could ask what he meant, he added, "We'll be landing soon."

Usually, talking about her family would make her stomach ache, but somehow it hadn't happened. In fact, it hadn't happened much since she'd got to Kalyana, despite the stress she'd been under. But she was glad he didn't pursue the conversation about her family further.

But then he said, "Sara, thank you for trusting me enough to tell me that story. I think..." He hesitated, just for a moment, then said, "We've become friends, haven't we, over these weeks?"

Her eyes got misty, and she turned her face

toward the side window so he wouldn't see. "Yes. I think we have too."

And acknowledging that fact once more made her consider taking him as her lover, and she kept her face turned away from him to hide the blush that rushed to her cheeks.

CHAPTER NINE

THE ANGER IN his chest burned like lit coals.

How could someone be that unkind to a child? Their own granddaughter, albeit an adopted one? Bless her mother for not standing for it, for protecting Sara as best she could.

Yet Farhan could see, clearly, what those words had done to Sara. They explained her almost compulsive need to be of service to her family and, by extension, everyone else. Perhaps without that horrible experience she might not be the person she was today, but he wished with all his heart she hadn't had to go through it anyway.

What she'd said about his father was something he'd have to think about later. It felt strange to be forced to see his father in a different light, think of him as a young, frightened boy who had probably lost his father to the throne and needs of Kalyana. But, again, if what she said was true, it too would explain much.

Right now, though, Farhan was solely focused on Sara, and the surprise he'd planned for her. Watching her these last couple of weeks, he'd seen her exhaustion. She'd been thrown into a life unlike any she'd known and it had taken its toll. Little bags had formed under those wide, expressive eyes, and while she'd treated everyone with her usual calm demeanor, Farhan had been aware of her knotted fingers and forced smiles.

And he doubted that being under constant scrutiny, especially now that she'd realized everyone was waiting for her to get pregnant, was helping her stress levels. So he'd arranged for them to have a couple of days away from it all at the royal villa on Agung before they started on their official tour. Set in fifty acres of woodland, right on the water, it was Farhan's favorite royal residence.

He wasn't sure why he'd kept it secret, and hopefully she wouldn't take it the wrong way. All he wanted was to give her a chance to relax, to be herself, in one of the most beautiful places he knew. There was no ulterior motive on his part, and he hoped she'd realize that.

As Agung came into view in the distance, he said, "There it is."

And he turned to watch her expression as she saw the island for the first time, wasn't disappointed when her eyes widened and her lips formed an "O" of surprise.

She gasped, leaning forward to see the island better, an emerald set in a sea shaded from cobalt through to aquamarine. "How gorgeous."

Her reaction warmed him.

"It's a beautiful island. Originally, it was a marine trading outpost for goods moving back and forth between Africa and Asia, and it's one of the most culturally diverse of the Kalyanese islands. When the marine trade dried up, the population declined, but now it's a popular tourist destination, and it's thriving again."

They were close enough to see the main town, and he banked the plane to give her a good view. It was built on a natural harbor, the colorful buildings flowing down off the surrounding hills toward the sea. Around a headland was a three-mile-long beach, dotted with low hotels and guest houses, mature trees keeping the landscape lush and green and contrasting with the huge granite boulders pushing up from the sea.

Sara turned to look out the side window as he passed over the town and tourist areas, continuing north.

"Wasn't that the airport back there?"

"Yes, but we're not landing there. The locals have planned an official welcome for us in a couple of days at Government House."

He could feel her gaze on him, even though he didn't take his eyes off the controls.

"So where are we going?"

The muscles in the back of his neck tightened. "There is a royal compound on the northwest side of the island. I thought you might enjoy a couple of days with absolutely nothing to do but laze around and relax, and there's nowhere better to do that than there."

She was silent for a moment and then, just when curiosity was about to make him turn to look at her, she exhaled.

"Thank goodness. I think that's exactly what I need."

And he quietly exhaled too, feeling as relieved as she sounded.

As the villa came into sight, he banked the

plane and did a fly over, to let Okello know they were there. Sara was leaning toward the window, craning her neck to see everything at once.

"Is that it? It's beautiful. What are those plants all along the hillside around the house?"

"Frangipani, and they give the villa its name."

"Gorgeous!"

Farhan found himself looking at the villa, which was a place he'd known his entire life, with new eyes. Through her enthusiasm, he felt his love for the land expand, grow along with his pride.

Villa Frangipani nestled among large flame trees on a promontory jutting out into the sea. The long slope of lawn from mansion to water was beautifully landscaped with swirls of the eponymous shrubs, now covered in waxy flowers. From above the house glowed like a pearl in the sun, and although it and the pool were clearly visible Farhan knew that once inside, veiled by the trees, there was an air of peaceful seclusion.

On the other side of the headland from their approach lay a smooth strip of pearl-pink sandy beach, sheltered from the rougher ocean waves by a reef and a dock. As he circled to come in for a landing on the smooth water, he saw Okello heading to the dock on the golf cart.

Touching down on the water and employing the flaps to slow the plane, he heard Sara give a little sigh of relief.

"Were you nervous?" he asked, smiling and sliding her a glance.

"Of course I was. I've never been on a seaplane; didn't even know you were a pilot."

"Good thing I knew what I was doing, then, huh?"

Her laughter filled the cockpit and, for some weird reason, his heart did as well.

More than ever before, he was looking forward to the next two days, telling himself it was strictly because they'd both have a chance to relax.

After all, why else would he be anticipating being practically alone with Sara?

Sara had never known her soul could sing, or that a place could make her feel so incredibly happy. The entire island of Agung had appeared lovely from the air but Villa Frangipani and its surroundings were perhaps the most glorious sight she'd ever seen, even in pictures. As Farhan helped her out of the plane onto the dock, the mingled scents of sea and flowers went to her head, and she had to fight the urge to laugh out loud in joy.

"Are you okay?"

Farhan was still holding her hand from when she'd taken his to step from the rocking plane, and she squeezed his fingers.

"More than okay," she replied, grinning up at him.

The quiet chug of an approaching vehicle attracted her attention and she turned to look, a little sorry when Farhan had to release her hand to close the plane door. A golf cart came down the gravel path from the house, then stopped at the end of the dock. A large, muscular man unfolded himself from it, rising to an impressive height before striding toward them.

Dressed in a brightly colored shirt and white cotton pants, his grin made his teeth appear dazzling white against his mahogany skin. He had strong features and kind, twinkling eyes.

"Your Highnesses."

He bowed over his hands, his voice surprisingly soft for such a huge man. Farhan stepped forward to shake the other man's hand, and then pulled him in for one of those male, back-slapping hugs.

"Okello. It's so good to see you."

"Farhan, yes, it's been too long, yeah? I thought you were avoiding me. Back a year and only just making it to Villa Frangipani."

Farhan gave a snort of laughter.

"You know how it is, my friend. Father keeps me on my toes."

"No doubt. No doubt."

Okello's gaze shifted to Sara, and she found herself being given a comprehensive once-over. Not that it made her feel uncomfortable. She thought she saw more curiosity than anything else in his dark, intelligent eyes.

"My wife, Sara. Sara, this is one of my oldest, dearest friends, Okello. He lives here and looks after the villa, while he's writing his novels."

"Nice to meet you, Okello." She held out her hand, and found it totally enveloped by his. "And, please, call me Sara."

His smile widened. "Thank you, Sara. I've been hearing about you on the news, and it's a pleasure to meet the woman who's willing to put up with Farhan."

She chuckled, not bothering to reply. She couldn't think of a single woman who'd toss Farhan out for eating crackers in bed, so she knew he was poking fun.

"Okay, that's enough." Farhan didn't sound particularly amused, even though he was still smiling. "Let's get the Princess up to the house."

While the men took the bags out of the plane and loaded them into the golf cart, Sara looked around, entranced by the scenery, deeply inhaling the fragrant air. This, more so than anything she'd experienced to that point, felt dreamlike, her heart seeming to beat in sync with the rush of the waves, every birdsong a symphony.

Was this what love at first sight felt like?

When Farhan put his hand on the small of her back to guide her toward the cart, it felt right in tune with her emotions. Looking up at him to smile, her heart skipped a beat when he smiled back, dipping his head as though about to kiss her, and her disappointment when he didn't was the only thing to mar her crazy happiness.

The ride up to the house passed quickly, Sara still taking in everything around her, captivated by the sight of the carefully pruned frangipani, with their blooms of cream or pink with yellow centers. The flowers looked like waxed satin, set against the deep green of the leaves. Filling in between the frangipani plants were lower bushes with small, light purple blooms, the entire effect one of tropical splendor.

The path led around the side of one wing of the two-story villa to the front door.

Farhan commented to her, "Normally when we're here we use the garden door to go in and out, especially when heading for the beach. Since this is your first time here, it'll be nice for you to see the house from the front and give you the official welcome."

It was only as they rounded the final corner that she realized the house was U-shaped, the two wings creating a central courtyard in front of the villa. A circular driveway looped around a fountain bearing the Kalyanese coat of arms with two dolphins leaping above. The entire effect was astoundingly beautiful.

Yet, although the outside of the villa was stately, the inside, while grand, was surprisingly soothing and comfortable. Instead of the gilded and elaborate ornamentation she'd grown used to at the palace, the Villa Frangipani was decorated in beige, white, and aqua, with pops of hot tropical colors as accents.

"My mother redecorated the house years ago, when we used to travel around as a family. Since my grandfather died it's hardly ever used for entertaining. Before then, he'd host polo parties here. Now if there's an official function, we use the Governor's residence. The villa is strictly for relaxing."

He led her up the curved staircase from the high-ceilinged entrance hall, into a huge, bright sitting room. Sara looked around, and then instinctively moved straight out through the open French doors onto the wide verandah beyond. From that vantage point she could see the pool below through the boughs of the flame trees and, in the distance, the glistening water of the ocean. A warm breeze tickled her playfully, working a few strands of hair loose from her bun to blow across her face, and birds called back and forth from the trees.

Spreading her arms wide, as though to embrace it all, she said, "This is paradise. I could live here forever and be absolutely happy."

"Me too," Farhan replied, a strange note in

his voice. Strange enough to make Sara spin to look at him.

His expression made her legs weak in an instant. Intent, his gaze, which was revealed by his having taken off his dark glasses, was the same as just before they'd kissed.

CHAPTER TEN

"MISHA WILL BE up to serve you lunch at one o'clock, so you have time to go swimming or snorkeling if you want."

Sara had been so focused on Farhan she hadn't noticed Okello coming up behind him, and from the way Farhan started, he hadn't noticed the other man either.

"Thank you," Farhan replied, not taking his eyes off Sara, leaving her shaken and suddenly completely aroused.

How could he do that with just a look?

"And Trinka was asking if you'll be coming by while you're here."

Who the heck was Trinka, and why did she expect a visit from him?

As Sara spun around to put her back to him, Farhan said, "Tell her I said hello, but I doubt I'll have time this visit. We'll be back soon, though."

Was it her imagination or did Farhan sound a

little curt? It wasn't like him, so Sara risked a glance over her shoulder and caught him giving his friend a glare.

"Okay. Give me a shout if you need anything."

Okello grinned before melting away as quietly as he'd appeared, and Sara quickly went back to staring at the scenery. The thrilling cord of awareness that had stretched between Farhan and her had been severed by the other man's arrival, and she wasn't sure whether to be happy about it or not.

"Hey, do you want to change into something cooler, or go for a swim?"

Ugh. She'd been dreading this moment from when it had first crossed her mind; Farhan seeing her in a swimsuit. Knowing he'd spent most of his adult life in Australia, she'd pictured him dating tall, willowy blondes like her sisters, and knew she couldn't compete in the body department. Yet what did it matter, in the grand scheme of things? Theirs wasn't a real marriage, so she shouldn't be silly about it.

Besides, the four swimsuits Mara had insisted she buy were all custom made and gorgeous. When she'd tried them on, even she'd thought she looked pretty good. She'd been dying to wear the emerald one. Whatever Farhan thought of her in it, he could go fly a kite.

But her internal pep talk didn't really help.

"A swim in the pool would be nice," she replied, trying for a distant tone, so as not to reveal her nervousness.

"We have snorkels and scuba gear if you'd rather go down to the beach. Do you scuba dive?"

The little snort broke from her lips before she could stop it. "I'd never even seen the ocean before coming on this trip, much less learned how to scuba dive. I think I'd like to go down to the sea, though, as long as it won't be boring for you."

"Of course not," he replied. "I love the sea. Let's get changed and head down."

They shared a suite in the northwest wing, consisting of a sitting room and two bedrooms, each with an en suite bathroom. Because of where the villa was built, all the bedrooms had wonderful sea views. On their shared balcony was a double-bed-sized swing, hung with sheer mosquito netting, suspended from the ceiling, and it called to her.

"There isn't one spot in this place that isn't perfect," she said, going over and trying it out immediately.

He came and stood beside the swing, a little smile playing around his lips.

"This place was a refuge for me, especially after Ali died, when I had to decide whether to follow what my father said, or give up my training and stay, the way I thought I should. But even before that, I'd spend most of my summers here, while my brothers traveled or stayed in Huban. There's something about the air here that makes all the colors brighter, and gives me so much peace of spirit."

On top of being gorgeous and a fine surgeon, he also had the soul of a poet.

How could she resist that combination?

Right then she wished he would come and lie on the swing with her, pull her close, kiss her again. Never before had kissing seemed so important to her, but with Farhan it took on a whole new importance. And never before had she wished she was more experienced when it came to men and how to seduce them.

Get a grip, Sara!

Jumping up off the swing, she said briskly, "Let's get going, so we aren't late for lunch."

They changed into swimsuits, packed the golf cart with all they'd need and drove it down to the beach. Once there, Sara fussed over which of the lounge chairs she'd use, putting her bottled water and towel on it before, in a little flurry of action, tugging off her cover-up and dashing into the sea. Running in until the water was deep enough, she plunged in up to her neck, amazed at how warm it was, in comparison to the lake water she was used to in Canada. There, even in summer, most of the lakes were cold.

Turning to say as much to Farhan, she was just in time to see him pull off his shirt.

The warm sea suddenly felt like it was boiling, or perhaps she was spontaneously combusting?

His back and arms rippled with muscles, and since he was wearing just his swim trunks she was also treated to the delectable sight of his strong legs and truly luscious butt. When he turned to walk toward the surf's edge, Sara's temperature rose another five degrees.

That chest!

Those abs!

The entire package should damn well be illegal.

Needing to cool off, she dipped her head under the water, uncaring that it would undo all the careful pampering Mara had been doing to her hair on an almost daily basis.

And came up spluttering.

"You okay?"

Farhan's voice was so close, Sara tried to open her eyes even before she'd properly wiped her face, and got another horrid surprise.

"Ugh, I didn't realize just how salty it would be. And it stings the eyes."

As she pushed back her hair, which was flopping in her face, gentle fingers wiped her eyes, and she opened them again to blink up at him, her breath catching in her throat at his nearness.

"You weren't kidding when you said you'd never been in the sea, were you?"

"N-no." She cleared her throat as best she could before continuing, "My parents would take us camping sometimes at the lakes, but never had money for vacations out of province."

"Hmm," Farhan said, reaching behind her head with one hand, the motion bringing him even closer. The action of the waves rocked their bodies together briefly, and Sara's insides melted. If he wasn't careful she was going to throw caution to the wind, reach up and grab him.

"You're about to start shedding hairpins."

Disappointment sliced through her arousal as she reached to take the errant pin from his hand, not knowing what she'd do with it.

Farhan held onto it, the brush of their fingers sending a zing of current through her skin.

"Let me," he said, sliding the pin onto the front of her suit, just above her right breast. "It should stay there."

She couldn't reply, trying as she was to keep her breathing level when his scent was filling her head and the innocent sensation of his fingers on her chest was giving her anything but innocent thoughts.

Then he reached both hands back behind her head, and started pulling the rest of the pins out of her hair.

No use trying to regulate her breath now, not with his chest lightly rubbing back and forth across her breasts, those gorgeous arms bracketing her head. And his lips, slightly pursed in concentration, were just within her eyesight, stealing her concentration for themselves.

"I've never seen you with your hair down, or in a bathing suit. It's a day for firsts."

His fingers were searching for any stray pins, and her entire scalp was tight and tingling from the attention, and it wasn't alone. Even through the padded swimsuit top, her breasts grew ever more taut with each brush of his chest, and delicious, unwanted lust heated her entire body even more. Sara bit the inside of her lip to stop the moan rising in her throat from escaping. If Farhan wasn't careful, she'd melt away to nothing, get washed out past the reef, and disappear.

Apparently satisfied that he'd removed all the pins, he gently untwisted her bun and fluffed her hair until it fell free.

Then, just when she thought her torture was through, he started putting the other pins with the first, warm fingers lightly running over her skin with each placement. Shivering despite the fire rampaging through her veins, she closed her eyes and felt as though she was floating away.

"I like this color on you. It suits you so well.

But, then, I've yet to see you look bad in anything you've worn."

That made her snicker, despite the arousal
careening through her body. At least having a
laugh would take her mind off his proximity,
right?

"Nobody looks good in scrubs," she coun-
tered, proud that she didn't stutter, although
there was a decided hitch in her voice.

"You do."

He really needed to stop saying those types
of things, or she'd just have to jump him.

"How about my ratty winter coat when we
first met?"

He didn't answer immediately, not until he'd
placed the final pin. Then he cupped her cheeks
and lifted her face so she was forced to meet
his gaze.

"Sara, the day you opened that door and I
saw you there, laughing at the dog, I thought
you beautiful. And I'm not saying that for any
reason other than it's true."

Again he stole her breath, and with it her
voice. His eyes were darker than usual, his face
stern, wreathed in what she'd always thought

of as arrogance but now wondered if it masked something else.

Farhan inhaled deeply, his lips firming briefly before he spoke again.

"I like you, think you're beautiful, smart, an amazing person. When my father instructed me to find you and marry you, I did it out of duty, but I couldn't be happier with the person I found when you opened that door."

Sara drew in a shaky breath, gob-smacked by his words, not knowing how to answer. But Farhan wasn't finished.

"I'm also very attracted to you, physically. Being around you all the time is difficult, because I want to touch you, kiss you, make love with you, but I don't know whether any of that is what you want."

He took another deep breath, and, if anything, his face got sterner.

"So I'm leaving it up to you to decide. If you want things to stay the way they are, with us as friends, then that's how they'll stay. Just let me know."

Her heart was pounding so fast her head spun, but she forced herself to breathe, slowly. Once. Twice.

His honesty was more effective than any soft words or calculated seduction could be. Knowing he wanted her, hearing him say it so plainly, made her want him even more in return.

Yet was it enough? Would she be able to share that kind of intimacy with him and walk away unscathed?

She wasn't sure, and until she could be, it would be wise to wait. But she owed him the same honesty he'd offered her, no matter how embarrassing it might be to admit.

Gathering her courage, and with a cold ball of fear gathering in her stomach, she said, "I'm not sure what I want, Farhan. The truth is, I've never slept with anyone before."

His eyes widened slightly, but he didn't pull away, just smoothed his thumbs over her still overheated cheeks.

"I didn't realize," he said. "But I'm glad you told me." Then his brow creased slightly. "Is there a reason for that? Religious, or—?"

"No," she replied quickly. "I just always thought of sex, and marriage too, to be honest, as something that would happen one day, sometime in a nebulous future I didn't give much thought to."

He nodded slowly, then bent and kissed her lightly on the cheek.

"Then I was doubly right to say you have to make the choice, especially since I suspect beneath it all, the real reason you waited is probably far more romantic in nature."

She considered that, searching within herself, then said, "If you mean I wanted to be in love before sleeping with someone, I hadn't given it much thought. I wanted a connection, to be attracted, of course, but really I was simply too busy with school, and then work, and my family to put in the effort relationships need. As for marriage, yes, I always thought I'd fall in love before taking that step, but here we are."

Farhan's lips tilted at the edges. Not a smile but something gentler. Almost tender.

"Yes, here we are." For a moment she thought he wouldn't say any more but, with that characteristic lift of his chin, he continued. "But if you decide to take this further, you know what to expect. I can't promise you something I don't have to give."

He meant love. She didn't want his love anyway, so it was moot.

Or was it?

She pushed that thought away and gently disengaged from his hold. Then she stepped back, needing some distance so she could start processing all he'd said.

Farhan's arms dropped to his sides and he smiled, but she thought there was a hint of sadness in his eyes.

"I'll think about what you've said, Farhan. And…"

He waited patiently while she sorted out exactly what she wanted to say. Everything they'd spoken about swirled in her head, but there were a couple of things that stood out.

They were, indeed, friends, despite the strange way they'd met, their sham of a marriage, and having him acknowledge that filled her with happiness.

Secondly, he was allowing, no, insisting she take the lead in whatever happened next between them. The relief she felt was heady.

Finally, she found the words she needed, the most important, which she'd almost forgot to say.

"Thank you."

CHAPTER ELEVEN

FARHAN MADE A concerted effort to put aside the seriousness of their talk in the water and, after a short time, Sara seemed to do so too. It felt amazing to be away from the official business of state, the life and death stress of their medical practices, and just enjoy the sun and surf.

Just before one o'clock they packed up the cart and went back up to the villa, where they found Okello's daughter, Misha, had the table set and lunch ready.

"Your Highnesses," she said, when they walked into the dining area, but then she grinned and gave Farhan a huge hug. "Uncle Farhan, it's been too long."

Farhan held her by the shoulders, giving her a searching look. "When did you receive royal permission to get so grown up, Misha? Didn't I specifically tell you to stay five years old forever?"

The young woman just laughed, and set about serving their meal—a simple one of deliciously prepared fish, vegetables, and tomato rice—all the while answering Farhan's questions about school and her plans for the future.

Then she slipped away, telling them to ring for her if they needed anything.

It was just the way he'd requested, since he'd wanted a completely relaxing couple of days, without people hovering over them all the time. It was a rare enough occurrence to be refreshing.

Just as they finished lunch, there was the slam of a door downstairs and then pounding footsteps. Okello came through the door like a torpedo.

"Farhan, Trinka just called. A retaining wall collapsed on one of the workers and she's asking if you'd come. It'll take the ambulance at least twenty minutes to get there."

He was on his feet in an instant, tossing his napkin onto the table.

"Do you know how badly hurt he is?"

"No. They were still digging him out when she called." Okello was already heading to the staircase as he spoke. "I'm going to get the car. Pick you up at the side door."

"Sara, I'll be right back," Farhan said, turning and realizing she was already on her feet too, and halfway to their suite.

"I'll come with, since you don't know how severe his wounds are, and an extra pair of trained hands might come in handy."

It was said over her shoulder, as she went through the door into the hallway beyond.

"Five minutes," he called out after her, hurrying to catch up and go change, glad she was going with him, hoping she'd be ready by the time Okello got back.

She was, with two minutes to spare, although she had her sneakers in one hand, medical bag in the other, and her hair was twisted into a rather precarious knot.

Hopping on first one foot and then the other, she got her shoes on just as Okello's SUV came barreling down the drive.

They scrambled in, and the vehicle was in motion again almost before the doors closed.

"Where did it happen?" Farhan asked.

"Back behind the grooming shed. Trinka noticed the other day that a tree up on the hillside was pushing out some of the rocks, so she decided to cut it down and repair the wall. I'm not sure what happened after that."

They rocketed through the gates, which Okello must have called ahead to have open, and turned onto the park, not toward the main road but north on a gravel side road. Farhan glanced back to see Sara trying to better secure her hair, now unruly after her swim.

The memory of taking down her hair and clipping the pins to her swimsuit tried to insinuate itself into his head, and Farhan had to make a concerted effort to push it away.

"Sara, seatbelt," he said, earning himself a mischievous glance from beneath her long, dark lashes.

"Yes, Dad," she muttered, even as she reached for the strap.

And somehow the frown he tried to send her for her teasing turned into a grin.

Sara appreciated the seatbelt when Okello took a corner on what she was sure was two wheels. She had no idea where they were going, but it didn't matter. What was important was that they get to the trapped worker as quickly as possible. Know that made the sticky feeling of her scrubs rubbing on salty skin bearable.

She'd debated whether to bring scrubs on their trip. After all, she wasn't just Dr. Greer anymore but Crown Princess, and people expected her to dress the part. However, since she'd be talking to women in clinics, it seemed less threatening to present herself the way they expected a doctor to dress, rather than all dolled up.

Now she was glad she'd decided to bring a few pairs, since it definitely sounded as though they were in for a dirty job.

The land they were driving through seemed untouched, large trees close together, covered in vines, with thick undergrowth. Wondering whether they were still on Villa Frangipani land, Sara stuck the last of the pins into her hair, hoping they would hold it up. Mara had a way of taming Sara's hair that Sara herself envied. She'd fought her hair all her life, only growing it out after she'd found a West Indian hairdresser in Toronto who'd helped her learn how to control it. But that was Canada, and this was Kalyana, where the humidity, no matter how light, made every strand want to do its own thing.

And now she knew seawater wasn't her friend either.

Thank goodness Farhan had stuck her hairpins onto the front of her suit, where she was able to grab them when she needed them.

Remembering him doing it, his face focused and intent, his fingers brushing her skin, made her heat through and through all over again.

Everything he'd said played in her mind.

He liked and was attracted to her.

Wanted her.

But wasn't in love with her.

The latter was fine. Like him, she'd never been in love, but she was pretty sure what she was feeling was lust, nothing more. He was gorgeous and a nice man, not the arrogant ass she'd thought him to be at first. Was that enough to make her sleep with him? It certainly was tempting. A chance like this might never come again.

They got to the top of a hill, went around another bend and there, in a little valley, was what she assumed to be their destination. The compound was encircled by a stone wall with a wooden gate, there were about six or so buildings and, in an area encircled with chain-link fencing...

"Dogs!"

She leaned forward to get a better look, noting the solid buildings, all clean and brightly painted.

"It's an animal sanctuary," Okello explained, as he pressed the accelerator hard, pushing the vehicle to go as fast as possible down the hill.

There was no time to ask any more questions as they roared through the gate to follow the drive around the buildings to the far corner of the compound, where a group of people had gathered.

Jumping out of the now stopped SUV, Sara reached in to grab her medical bag and ran after Farhan and Okello, who had a head start on her.

The crowd parted, and Sara's stomach dropped when she saw the pile of stones men were frantically pulling away from the still body barely visible beneath them.

Farhan got to the man's head first, with Sara right behind him.

To her shock, when she knelt down beside him, she saw the man's eyes were open, aware, although shadowed with pain. Farhan was already doing his assessment, so Sara decided to be his back-up, listening and taking note of all the man said in response to questions. Opening her bag, she took out and put on a pair of gloves, and then, using antiseptic solution and soft gauze, started cleaning up the young man's face. From her visual inspection, she suspected his nose was broken, and there was a gash above his right eye, which she wanted to check the severity of. While there was a flap of skin hanging down over his eyebrow, and copious bleeding, as was usual with head wounds, her opinion was that it was minor, although there could be concussion.

Farhan was examining the young man, who said his name was Nolan, asking him how the accident had happened while gently inspecting his head and neck. His pupils looked normal, his color surprisingly good for someone stuck under a pile of rocks. Sara looked to see the progress of the other men, still heaving stones away, and was glad to see Nolan's chest was almost free.

"I was below the wall, sir, marking where it

needed to be repaired, when I heard the stones creaking. I tried to run, but tripped and fell."

"There's a drainage ditch just about here, isn't there? Did you fall into that?"

"I'm not sure, sir."

At least he was lucid and, although having to breathe through his mouth because of his broken nose, didn't seem to be in major distress.

Farhan looked up at her. "Do you have a neck brace in your kit?"

"No," she replied.

"Then unless it's absolutely necessary to move him, I think we should leave him here until the ambulance arrives."

Sara nodded and as the last of the stones over Nolan's chest and abdomen were removed, she shifted so Farhan could take his examination lower.

It was almost miraculous. Nolan professed to feel no pain in his back, chest, or abdomen, but as they pulled the last of the stones away, Sara's heart sank. His leg was twisted under him at an abnormal angle, obviously either broken or badly dislocated at the knee.

The sound of a siren in the distance was a huge relief. There really wasn't much either Farhan or she could do under the circumstances, and without the right equipment.

She made a mental note to get a larger medical bag and stock it with a neck brace for any future emergencies. Not that she was hoping for any more excitement like this. The whole situation made her painfully aware of how sheltered her medical experience really had been to that point. Working in the field, without the amenities she was used to having at her fingertips, was nerve-racking.

Farhan turned to a woman standing on the sidelines, her arms wrapped around her waist, a worried expression on her weathered face.

"Is there an orthopedic surgeon at the hospital? His leg is going to need surgery."

"Yes. Dr. Ronan. I hear he's good."

The ambulance arrived, and Farhan brought the supervisor up to speed on all he'd seen. Then he fitted Nolan's neck and back braces himself, and made sure no one tried to straighten the young man's leg.

"It's definitely dislocated, and it needs to be dealt with at the hospital."

"Yes, sir."

Poor Nolan tried to be brave, but the pain

from his leg had him groaning and swearing as they transferred him to a gurney.

Stripping off her gloves, Sara watched the ambulance pull away. Farhan was standing with the woman he'd asked about the surgeon, deep in conversation, and she didn't want to interrupt. Then they walked over to her, and the woman held out her hand.

"Your Highness, I'm Trinka Daniels, and I'm in charge of this crazy place. Thank you for coming to help Nolan."

"It's nice to meet you, Trinka," she said politely, taking the outstretched hand and getting a firm handshake.

"Well, since you're here, Farhan, do you want to nose around and see what we've been up to since you last visited? It's been a while, and although I keep you updated, it's different when you can see it all for yourself. Take the Princess with you, while I supervise feeding time."

They ended up spending most of the rest of the afternoon at the sanctuary, which Sara learned Farhan had set up himself.

Something else she hadn't known about him; another facet in his complex personality.

She couldn't resist wading into the pack of

dogs in the field, greeting all those that wanted attention, trying to coax a few of the shyer ones to come to her. Farhan had retreated into a businesslike demeanor, speaking mostly to Trinka and Okello, all but ignoring Sara. Yet, although he didn't speak to her directly more than two or three times, there were a great deal more times that she looked at him and found his gaze focused entirely on her.

And she couldn't help noticing how gentle and involved he was with the dogs who came to him, wanting affection.

"I'm glad to see the adoption numbers have been going up," he remarked to Trinka, who nodded.

"We've made quite a bit of headway in that regard, especially when it comes to the puppies. But I want to increase the number of older dogs we rehome, and get more people to foster dogs, to give them a bit of basic training, increase their socialization and chance of finding a forever home. A few of us have been talking about setting up a support animal training program too, but that's later on. None of us have the time or expertise right now."

Sara looked up from where she was sitting

cross-legged on a low wooden platform, three dogs draped over her lap, all wanting rubs at the same time.

"I know someone in Ottawa who's involved in the training of medical and emotional support animals. Whenever you're ready, let me know and I'll put you in touch with him."

"Him?" Farhan asked. His tone was mild, but the question made her want to blush for some reason.

"Yes. It's my Uncle Stanton, my dad's brother. Most of that side of the family is involved with animals in some way."

Thankfully, the conversation shifted to other topics, and Sara could concentrate on the little dog who'd won pride of place on her lap. Of indeterminate breed, he was a shaggy little fellow with big brown eyes peering from behind a floppy fringe.

"That's Coco, short for Coconut, and he normally doesn't go to people," Trinka remarked. "You obviously have the touch."

Stroking his wiry fur, Sara wished she had the wherewithal to take Coco when she left, but didn't say anything. Maybe before she went back to Canada, she'd come back and liberate him. Hopefully he wouldn't have to be quarantined back home. She'd look into it when it got closer to the time for her to leave.

Suppressing a sigh, she cuddled the dog a little closer, looking around at the verdant hills, tuning out the human conversation to focus on the birds, the whisper of breeze through the foliage. Canada seemed so very far away despite the constant contact with her family. It was a different life, and one that she didn't miss as much as she'd thought she would. Kalyana had a completely different rhythm, the country's heart beating at a slower rate, the people moving at a pace most Canadians would find unbearably leisurely.

Sara, however, was growing to love it all. Sitting here under a sky so blue it could make you cry, the sun warm on her head, there was nowhere she would rather be, and the thought of leaving it behind one day made her unbearably sad.

Coco sat up abruptly, whined under his breath, then reached up to lick her chin.

"Are you okay?"

She didn't notice Farhan moving until he stooped down next to where she was sitting.

The expression on his face was one she didn't remember ever seeing before. Was that concern tightening the skin around his eyes?

"Of course. Why?"

He shook his head. "You just looked…a little off."

She smiled at him, wanting so badly to smooth away the wrinkles between his brows, curling her fingers into Coco's fur to stop herself doing it.

"I'm fine. Really."

But leaving the little dog behind all but broke her heart, and on the way back to Villa Frangipani, she stared out the side window of the SUV, wondering when her life had gone from simple to so darned complicated.

CHAPTER TWELVE

SHE WAS STILL pondering that question while she showered and changed once they got back.

It was, of course, all about Farhan. He'd turned her life upside down, and not just because of his proposition. No, it was *him*. Him and the life he'd shown her here in Kalyana, a place that called to her heart just as he did.

The thought brought her up short, made a shiver run down her spine.

She couldn't fall for him. She just wouldn't.

Putting aside all his wonderful attributes, his stated attraction to her and the pleasure it gave her to know he wanted her, that would be the stupidest thing she'd ever done in her life. The year would fly by. And, when it was over, if she allowed herself to care for him in any way more than as a friend, the heartbreak would be immense.

She still wasn't sure she could sleep with him

and not get emotionally involved. Even Farhan's warnings didn't quell the intensity of her desire.

He'd told her the choice was hers, and he'd go along with whatever she decided.

She'd just have to make sure she didn't make the wrong choice.

No matter how hard that ultimately might be.

But Sara almost had to eat her own words when she stepped out onto the verandah and saw Farhan standing in the final glow of the setting sun. He was wearing a plain white kurta over pants of the same fabric, the soft linen doing nothing to conceal his wonderful physique. His hair was damp, and from where she stood, frozen, behind him, she could see his strong, wide-palmed hands gripping the balustrade.

Memories of those hands holding and caressing her crashed through her system, trailing fire in their wake. Her determination not to give in to her own lust had been made in the vacuum of solitude, somehow not taking into consideration the bone-deep effect that being in his presence had on her.

He turned then, as though sensing her standing there, and the look he gave her almost melted her on the spot.

It wasn't the sultry air making it impossible to breathe. It was the darkness of his gaze, the slight softening of his stern lips, the sensation of being pulled toward each other, although neither of them moved.

"Dinner is ready, Uncle Farhan."

Misha's voice from farther down the verandah broke the silent, heat-saturated moment between them, allowing Sara to take a breath into her oxygen-starved lungs.

"Come, beautiful." He gestured for her to precede him to the table set on the verandah, decorated with frangipani blossoms and candles sending flickering light over the crisp white cloth.

She couldn't reply, her voice still lost in the timeless, thrilling instant just gone.

He pulled out her chair, as he always did, and Sara braced herself for the proximity when slipping by him. But even so his subtle, delicious scent still went straight to her head.

The man was a walking intoxicant.

"I'm glad we had time to visit the animal shelter," Farhan said, during dinner. "There's another main one in the south, not as big as this one but with a wider variety of animals. Some horses, donkeys, goats, as well as dogs and cats. If we have time, we'll go."

It was the first time he'd mentioned the sanctuaries, and Sara now felt comfortable asking, "Trinka mentioned you'd set them up yourself, when you were in your teens. How did it all happen?"

He lifted one shoulder; a self-effacing gesture she'd come to recognize.

"I never got used to seeing all the stray dogs wandering the street. I used to bring some of them home to the palace, but my parents weren't too happy about that."

Sara chuckled, picturing the King and Queen realizing the palace was being overrun with strays.

"One day I picked up a stray, intending to take it home, but I found out it wasn't a stray at all. It actually belonged to someone who loved it very much but didn't have the wherewithal to properly care for it. The dog hadn't been neutered, so it was constantly in fights. It was riddled with worms, and showed signs of mange."

He wasn't looking at her as he spoke, but out into the moonlit gardens.

"I started paying for people to spay and neuter their animals, and told my father the government should do something about all the strays. He told me people come first, and if I wanted something done about it, then it was up to me. So I did, using some of my inheritance from my grandfather. But it's really the people running the sanctuaries and shelters who are doing all the work."

He said it so matter-of-factly, as though it were no big deal. His humbleness moved her in a soul-deep way.

"But you don't have any animals of your own?"

A fond smile, tinged with sadness, tipped the edges of his lips.

"I had two dogs in Australia, but they both died a couple of years ago. I haven't had the heart to get any more since. When I need a dog fix, I go and volunteer at the shelter in Huban."

"I love dogs too," she said, scooping up a bit of her crème brûlée, which was so delicious that each bite was like a symphony on her taste buds. "In fact, I'd like to take that little dog

Coconut back with me when I return to Canada. I'm not sure how that works, though. I'd hate for him to have to spend a long time in quarantine or anything."

The look he gave her was unfathomable, but he nodded. "We're rabies free, and have good contact with the Canadian government. I'm sure it can be arranged."

"Oh, thank you," she said, smiling across at him, happy in a way she couldn't remember being before.

Their gazes met, held, and the now-familiar heat flooded her system, until it felt as though warm honey flowed in her veins.

It was then, at that moment, she decided.

She wanted him, and she wanted him here, at Villa Frangipani, the most beautiful place in the world.

Now, if she could just figure out how to let him know without embarrassing herself in the process.

Why did he hate hearing her speak about returning to Canada? It wasn't as though he didn't know she was eventually going and, in fact, he was glad it was still foremost in her mind. In some ways he felt they were getting too close, speaking about subjects close to their hearts, while the way he really wanted to get intimate with her seemed unlikely to happen.

He wanted her in his bed, not his head. And definitely not in his heart.

Sara went quiet, not looking at him, and in the soft candlelight and moonlight it was impossible to read her expression.

Instead of trying to engage her, Farhan let his mind wander.

What she'd said about his father still nagged at him.

She'd been able to imagine the turmoil the child, suddenly second in line to an unwanted throne, must have felt. How the enmity of those around him, along with how busy his father had been while putting the country to rights, must have affected him, scarred him in a fundamental way.

It certainly explained his distance and sternness, and the obsession with the missing Bhaskar, which had set Farhan and Sara on this strange path together. What else about his father, who Farhan had often thought of as a cypher, could that explain?

Recalling the conversation that had led to her comment just made his blood boil all over again. Her grandmother had treated her abominably, yet Sara had held no grudge. Indeed, she was actively involved in the old woman's care, and he remembered her even feeding her at dinner while the rest of the family did nothing to help.

Sara was so giving. Too giving. Was she still trying to prove her worth to her family, and now to the people of Kalyana? She'd been distressed by people requesting her patronage for various charities and causes, asking his advice.

"Anyone who approaches you directly, tell them to send an official request, in writing, outlining the work the charity does, and the role they envision you playing, along with last year's financial statement. I'll get Seth to collate it all, as well as doing due diligence to make sure they're above board, then you can decide."

"But I won't be here very long, Farhan. I don't want to accept a role I won't be able to fulfill in the future."

"Then don't accept any of them," he'd said, in

what he'd thought was a reasonable response, but Sara had just looked more distressed.

"But I want to help," she'd said softly.

They'd talked about it some more, without being able to come to a firm decision, but it was so clear to him: Sara would give everything to everyone around her, perhaps to her own detriment.

Dinner finished, he suggested a walk on the beach, but she declined.

"I—I think I'd prefer to stay u-up here," she stammered, and he saw a blush rise to her cheeks. It sharpened his focus, had him drawing closer to her so as to see the expression in her eyes.

And when she twined her arms around his neck and tilted her face up to his, his body reacted with a surge of arousal so strong he was instantly hard.

"May I kiss you?" she asked, her voice breathless, a little unsure.

CHAPTER THIRTEEN

FARHAN'S EXPRESSION CYCLED from surprise to desire in a tick of a heartbeat.

Then his mouth was on hers, the kiss urgent, compelling her lips to open instinctively, a moan rising in her throat as her insides melted, lust flashing out like a wildfire.

With the last of her functioning brain she gave thanks that he hadn't asked for an explanation, hadn't made her tell him why she'd had this abrupt change of heart.

From the moment they'd met the attraction she felt was more intense than she'd ever imagined possible, and it had only grown stronger with each passing day.

He was only hers for a little while. So much time had already gone by. This was her opportunity to do exactly what she'd secretly hoped all her adult life.

Share herself, on the most intimate level, with

someone she cared about. It didn't matter if he didn't care as much.

This was for her.

Farhan pulled her closer, and she let her hands roam his back, the thin linen of his kurta doing nothing to stop her from tracing the muscles but annoying her nonetheless.

She wanted to feel his bare skin, learn, once and for all, if it was as smooth as it looked.

Pressed against his chest, she wallowed in the exquisite sensations turning her insides to lava, burning for him in a way she'd never thought herself capable of. This level of want, of sheer unadulterated need, was beyond her wildest imaginings, but it didn't frighten her at all. If anything, it only made her more determined to take this moment to the ultimate conclusion.

How could she live with herself after she left Kalyana if all she took with her were regrets rather than beautiful memories?

Memories of making love with Farhan.

Farhan lifted his head and she stood on tiptoes, trying to re-establish the kiss.

"Wait." It was a growl, the strain in his voice so obvious she shivered with the knowledge she affected him that way. "Sara, you have to tell me when to stop. I want you so badly, you'll have to tell me if I go too far."

Her heart, already racing, seemed to trip over itself, and she swallowed to clear her throat before she could reply.

"I'll tell you, Farhan."

But she had no intention of telling him to stop. She wanted to experience everything he could give.

Leading him upstairs to her bedroom didn't seem too daunting; knowing what to do when they got there was another thing altogether.

Thankfully, Farhan took over, pulling her back into his arms as soon as the door closed behind them.

"Sara." Her name sounded like a benediction when he said it. "Beautiful."

Her knees weakened, her body tightening in anticipation as he found her lips once more.

Then they were on the bed, still fully clothed, and she lost herself in the wonder of his kisses again.

Yet eventually she realized he wasn't taking it any further. Not that kissing him wasn't thrilling, but she wanted more.

And realized she was going to have to ask for it.

She didn't know the words. Didn't know how people navigated situations like this. But if she wanted to make love with Farhan, she was going to have to put her shyness and fear aside, and let him know.

They were lying side by side, one of his hands on her ribcage, the other lost somewhere among the pillows. Would it be enough to simply shift his hand up to cover her breast?

That would be a small step, and she wasn't in the mood for those.

Before he realized what she was about to do, she rolled away from him and sat up.

She heard his indrawn breath, felt him run a finger gently down her back.

No doubt he thought she was putting a halt to their lovemaking and, for a moment, she froze, terrified by what she was planning to do.

She got up off the mattress, and turned to face him, and the sight of him stole her breath, had shivers of lust coursing down her spine. His hair was mussed from her fingers running through the strands, his eyes still dark with passion, his lips soft from her kisses. It felt so right to see him in her bed, one leg bent so the foot was flat on the mattress, the other canted to one side, his erection clearly delineated beneath his clothing.

She reached for the side zipper of her dress and it was then she realized her fingers were shaking, but she willed them to get the simple chore done.

His gaze followed the motion of her hand as she tugged the zipper down to her hip, then snapped up to her face as she slid her arms out of the dress, letting it fall to the carpet.

Her toes curled at his expression, her temperature skyrocketing at the mingled shock and need on his face.

"Sara…"

It was a warning and an invitation, all in one, but she ignored the former, knowing it was the latter that was important.

You can do this, Sara.

But her fingers weren't just shaking, they were also ice cold as she reached back to unclip her bra. When her breasts swung free, she gasped, heat suffusing her chest and face at exposing her body to him so boldly.

Suddenly she realized she didn't know what

to do next. Just the thought of taking off her panties froze her in place, and she only just stopped herself from crossing her arms over her chest.

And there was nowhere to run. This was, after all, her room.

Farhan sat up. Then he pulled off his shirt, and Sara's breath caught deep in her chest at how gorgeous he was.

Holding out his hand, he said, "Come here, beautiful."

And all her fear and trepidation disappeared as she went to him.

There was something dreamlike in how Farhan touched her; the slow drag of his fingers over her skin, the play of his mouth on hers. Although she'd clearly shown him she was ready, no, eager for his possession, he was in no rush to get there.

"Beautiful," he murmured into her flesh, and she didn't know whether he was using it as a proper noun—his nickname for her—or an adjective, and didn't care. She was too lost in these new, entrancing sensations to worry about it.

His fingers stroked over her breasts, bringing

her nipples to tight oversensitive peaks, his lips dipped from her mouth to her throat. Her body bowed, arousal pulling it tighter and tighter.

"Beautiful."

When the tip of his tongue swirled around her nipple, Sara whimpered, her fingers finding the back of his head to hold him in position, loath to let him stop the sweet torture.

But he had just begun to introduce her to the world of passion, and each touch and lick and kiss ushered her into new realms of desire.

His lips on the inside of her elbow, his mouth on her stomach. Neither of these were actions she would have associated with the act of sex, or with foreplay. In life outside these four walls, she never would've considered they could make her body twist with wanton need.

Yet when Farhan kissed from her shoulder to her wrist, her rushed breathing hitched, and she pressed her thighs together, the ache between them building toward unbearable.

The heat of his mouth on her breast, the sweet drag of his palm on its mate brought her back off the mattress, little cries of sweet, agonizing craving breaking, unfettered, from her lips.

Then he moved lower, and she trembled at

the slow, concentrated flicking of his tongue, as it traced back and forth over her abdomen.

"Farhan…" she whispered, her throat too dry to allow anything louder.

He lifted his head, and in the darkness of his gleaming eyes she saw a hint of the pleasure to come.

"Is this enough, beautiful? Do you want me to stop?"

If he stopped now, she might lose her sanity. "No. No."

His face tightened, became almost feral, and her heart rejoiced to see it.

"How much further do you want me to go, Sara? I need to know."

She understood. He was asking how much restraint he needed to build up. It made her adore him even more, knowing he would go as far as she said and no further, regardless of his own needs.

It gave her the courage to say what she truly wanted, out loud, making it clear to them both.

"I want to make love with you," she said.

And there wasn't even a hint of a stutter in her voice.

He gazed at her for a long moment, the air

between them heavy with passion, and then he said, "I want to make love with you too, but my initial promise still stands. If you want to stop, at any point, tell me."

Unable to resist, she reached down and cupped his face, curling down so as to kiss him, long and deep.

"I won't change my mind," she murmured against his lips. "I want you so badly, I'm burning up inside."

His lips curled into a smile as she lay back down, and he replied, "I'm glad, for I feel the same way. I'll be right back. Don't move."

Rising quickly, he strode to the connecting door between their rooms, but was gone only for a minute. When he returned, it was to toss a small, foil-wrapped package onto the nightstand, and Sara mentally kicked herself for not thinking of protection first. Thank goodness one of them had the presence of mind to do so.

Lying back down in the same position he'd been in before, Farhan dipped his head to kiss a slow trail down her belly and then around her navel, Sara's entire body trembled with delightful anticipation. Rising to his knees, he traced a finger across the top of her panties.

"May I?"

She lifted her hips in reply, although a fresh wave of trepidation washed over her skin.

Farhan eased her last garment away, his fingers caressing her legs. Lifting her left leg, he kissed her ankle, stroking his tongue across the sensitive skin beneath her medial malleolus. Up her leg that sinful mouth travelled, until he was at her knee. Then he turned his attention to her other leg, repeating every enticing action.

Suddenly Sara realized her feet were on his shoulders, her previously most private flesh fully open to his view.

Even if she were inclined to feel self-conscious, Farhan's avid expression would have swept the emotion away.

"I want to taste you."

It was statement and question rolled into one, and Sara replied by spreading her thighs a little wider, placing her hand on her belly, inviting him to take whatever he wanted.

He swooped down, and Sara cried out at the intensity of feelings bombarding her system, the unbelievable sensory overload. Her body shook, strung tight with lust from just the first touch of his tongue, his lips. Farhan held her hips, slowing his tender assault, taking her higher and higher, easing her toward an indefinable golden moment she could sense nearing. Her thighs tightened around his head, as she strained to reach that final glorious treasure.

"Easy," he murmured, not lifting his head, so that the word itself pulled her a little closer. "Relax, beautiful. Let it happen."

She wanted it, the orgasm tempting her beyond reason, but, lost in a maze of previously unknown physical delight, something held her back. Fear, carnal excess, inexperience, she didn't know which, but whatever it was, it was driving her slowly crazy.

"Farhan, please. Help me."

He growled, a low sound of need as great as her own, and his hands tightened fractionally.

"Do you trust me, Sara?"

How could he ask such a thing at a time like this? But she was compelled to whimper, "Yes."

"Then let me love you, beautiful. Let me make this good for you."

Opening her eyes, she looked down at him, his handsome face bracketed by her thighs, and the sight made her gasp. It was so intimate, reflecting a physical closeness she'd never shared with anyone before, and somehow it both increased her arousal and loosened her muscles.

Because it was Farhan. The only man she'd ever wanted this way. The only one she'd trust with her body, and knew she'd never regret doing so.

"Good," he growled and then, as she watched, he flicked her with the tip of his tongue.

And she exploded into ecstasy.

Sara's sweet cries of release echoed through Farhan's blood, pushing his own almost painful desire even higher.

Her gorgeous body twisted as he kept her orgasm going, not stopping until she pushed his head away. Then he covered her trembling flesh with his hand, gentling her until her breathing settled slightly, and her muscles started to relax.

But he didn't want her completely satiated, not if she'd meant it when she'd said she wanted to make love with him.

No. He wanted her as ravenous for him as he was for her.

He quickly divested himself of his remaining garments, and moved up to hold her. Yet, even in the tender moment, he let his hands keep touching her, finding the places that had made her gasp with desire before, slowly rousing her back to a state of need.

He craved her kisses, took her mouth over and over. Then he moved to her sensitive neck, kissing, nibbling, licking, until those sweet little gasps and moans rang out again.

He didn't want to hurt her. That was his one worry. Her inexperience was there, hovering in the back of his mind, even as his carnal self fought for supremacy, urging him to take her hard and fast.

Sara may be the true virgin, but in a way he felt like one as well, having never *had* a virgin in his bed. It filled him with a kind of masculine pride he'd never have credited himself with being in possession of, but also weighed him down with a sense of responsibility too.

Sensing it was time, and even after rolling on the condom, Farhan still hesitated. Eventually it was Sara who pulled him close, wrapping her strong legs around him and rolling so he lay atop her, perfectly positioned.

"Wait," he growled, his body tense with the drive to thrust into her. "I want to be sure—"

"I'm sure," she replied, her voice strained, passion-drunk. "I can't wait anymore. Please."

He tried to go slowly, every muscle locked, tenderness his touchstone. But the sublime encounter was also an irrevocable one, and they both knew it. Her eyes were open, looking up into his, and although he wanted to close his in rising ecstasy, he kept his gaze locked on hers, searching for any hint of pain or uncertainty.

There was none.

She welcomed him into her body, accepted him, just as his heart had welcomed and accepted her advent into his life.

The knowledge fired through him, rendering the moment sweeter, hotter, with an edge of incipient pain he didn't know how to process.

Holding still to allow her body time to accept his, he watched her eyes flutter closed, even as her hips shifted restlessly beneath his. Still he didn't move, caught in the transcendent intimacy. Sara's gorgeous neck was arched, her face was flushed and damp, her lips slightly parted, the breath rushing between them.

She was perfect. Perfect for him. And the urge to declare her his, to put his stamp on her for all to see, was almost overwhelming. Nothing he'd ever experienced before had prepared him for this.

For making love to a woman, instead of merely seeking sexual release.

"Farhan…"

He loved how she said his name, both question and demand, her voice gravelly with desire; acceded to the demand and answered the question with long, slow thrusts. Her short nails dug into his back, and she shuddered again and again.

"Yes," she whimpered. "Oh, yes."

Her responsiveness was almost his undoing, and he had to pause to regain some semblance of control.

"Don't stop," she moaned. "Oh, Farhan, don't stop."

He was losing his grip, ready to spiral into orgasm, and he didn't want to go alone. Heaving to his knees, he pulled Sara closer, seating himself fully inside her. She gasped, her legs locking around his waist, her fingers gripping the sheet on either side of her hips.

Then he reached down, found her clitoris with his thumb, as he began to thrust again.

She came apart, crying out his name, and it was all he needed to follow her into bliss.

CHAPTER FOURTEEN

THE DAYS THAT followed were the best of Sara's life.

While in public Farhan's behavior toward her didn't change, at night he was the lover she hadn't known she'd wanted, but now realized she'd always dreamt of.

Tender, attentive to her needs, fiercely arousing her and making sure satisfaction was achieved, for them both. In her case, multiple times.

It was like being caught up in an erotic fantasy, and whenever he said, "Come here, beautiful," she knew the dream was about to come true, again.

The only incident that could have marred her happiness came the day after they'd made love for the first time, and she'd screwed up the courage to say, "If we're going to continue sleeping together, you're going to keep needing to use protection, always. Or at least until I can get back to the hospital and go on the Pill."

Farhan's face was expressionless as he surveyed her for a couple of long seconds, but his chin tipped up in that habitual, arrogant look he had. Then it seemed as though he would speak, but stayed silent.

When he didn't answer, Sara continued, "Farhan, you don't want a child, and neither do I under these circumstances."

His lips firmed into a thin line, then he replied, "Of course."

Then he changed the subject, speaking about the rest of their tour.

The switch to something so impersonal made Sara's stomach dip, and she'd wondered if she'd ruined the sexual closeness they'd only just found. But she shouldn't have worried. That night Farhan had come to her room, lightly knocking on the connecting door, not entering until she'd called out for him to do so.

"Would you welcome my company?" he'd asked, solemn-faced, his eyes watchful.

And, of course, she'd said yes.

She wanted all she could get of Farhan while she still could.

Seated at the vanity, she'd been brushing out her hair when he'd entered, and Farhan had come to stand behind her, his gaze intent on her reflection.

"I like it when your hair is down," he'd said quietly, as he'd taken the brush from her hand. "Why don't you leave it down more often?"

"It's very hard to handle, and the humidity here tends to make it go a little nuts. Even Mara has trouble getting it to behave."

He stroked the brush through so gently, she felt tears sting the backs of her eyes, and was glad he was concentrating on what he was doing, rather than on her face. It was a surreal, fairy-tale type of moment, and for once she felt she belonged in such a situation. Something about Kalyana had changed her, made her more confident, able to deal with whatever came her way.

"May I sleep in here with you tonight?" he asked quietly, still not looking at her face.

"I hoped you would," she replied.

And when their gazes met then in the mirror, a wave of need and happiness made her smile up at him.

* * *

Leaving Villa Frangipani felt like being torn away from Paradise, but it was time to return to reality, and the job at hand, at least during the day. Joined by Kavan, Mara, and Seth, they started there in Agung.

While their main mission was to survey the women on the various islands regarding their medical needs, there were also a lot of official functions they were expected to attend. It became an exhausting excursion, but at night all her fantasies continued to come true and that made it bearable.

She'd hoped taking their relationship to a physical level would somehow cool her ardor but, instead, Sara's attraction to Farhan grew more intense each day. She found herself watching his hands, his face, noticing the way he walked, hoarding the memory of each smile.

To take her mind off her obsession with Farhan, at least some of the time, she threw herself into interacting with the women, finding it incredibly informative and interesting.

"In truth, I don't think we need a women's clinic," one lady told Sara, when she visited a local hospital on one of the north central islands. "Rather, it would be better if we simply had more female doctors available at the hospital and rural clinics."

That seemed to be the general consensus among most of the women she spoke to. Some said that while dedicated women's clinics would be nice, recruiting more female practitioners would be just as effective.

By the time they were halfway through their tour, Sara felt she had a good handle on how the women felt, and reported their concerns to Farhan. He listened to her and then nodded.

"There is a disproportionate number of male doctors recruited to work here, and I'm not sure why that is. It's something worth looking into."

She knew there was no medical school in Kalyana, and many of their medical practitioners were recruited from other countries. "Are there grants, programs to encourage young women to study medicine abroad and then come back here to practice? That would be the best option, since they'd be returning to their own land, already knowing the culture, rather than bringing in strangers. And if grants are too expensive, set it up in such a way that they can work off their med school fees over time. Then they'd have a real incentive to come back."

They were sitting outside after dinner at another of the royal family's residences, this one a miniature fortress in the hills on one of the central islands. The Governor had explained that when the British had used the main town as a transshipment point, there had been periodic outbreaks of malaria because of the swampy land surrounding the port. With there being fewer mosquitos at higher elevations, they'd built the fortress to retire to, a place where they could feel secure even when in poor health. It had become a royal residence once the British had left.

It still retained the aura of its colonial past, with dark heavy furniture and overstuffed chintz-covered chairs and sofas, nothing like any of the other residences Sara had seen. Yet it also had a timeless quality she liked, harkening back to the past, untouched by the often seen need to ruthlessly drag everything into modernity. Sitting on a comfortable love seat, Farhan beside her, holding her hand and playing with her fingers, Sara was enjoying the cool, fragrant mountain air.

"Again, something to look into. I know there are a handful of scholarships handed out each year, but perhaps setting one up that's strictly for young women would be useful."

"And ensure girls are encouraged to study sciences in schools. I know Kalyana is fairly progressive and egalitarian when it comes to women's rights, but even in North America there are still ingrained biases against it. Maybe you should also think about what it would take to set up a university, so young people don't have to leave the country to study in the first place."

If she had been going to remain in Kalyana, that would be a cause she'd get involved with. But she wasn't, as she had to keep reminding herself. For once she felt as though she was where she belonged, and just the thought of leaving opened a hole in her chest.

It had nothing to do with Farhan, she told herself stoutly. While his lovemaking was amazing, catapulting her into the sexual stratosphere, there was no place in their relationship for emotion. She wouldn't allow herself to care for him, knowing it would be completely one-sided. Part of what made the intimacy between them work was both of them knowing it was safe, and neither would make things difficult.

She was on a journey of discovery, learning new things about herself, her desires and ambitions. And what she found was truly eye-opening.

Far from being the passive mouse she'd always assumed herself to be, she'd realized hidden strengths, especially in bed with Farhan. She wasn't content to let him always take the lead, set the pace. Learning his body, what turned him on and made him wild, became a mission of sorts, one she embraced with gusto.

His ears were particularly sensitive, and his back was one big erogenous zone, which she put to good use. Even on occasion in public, which, as she surreptitiously ran a finger down it, earned her some stern looks from him, making her hard pressed to contain giggles.

He'd acceded to her wishes, and they always used condoms. And when one night she'd taken the little packet from his hand and offered to put it on for him, the way his face tightened told her volumes.

After that it became a part of their play, an island of quiet in the storm of their lovemaking, although no less arousing for the tenderness of it.

"You make me lose myself," he said to her one night, as she carefully smoothed on the prophylactic, and coming from the contained, controlled Farhan, it filled her with joy.

Their tour was coming to an end, and Sara wasn't sure if she were happy about it or not. They'd been somewhat freer while traveling than they'd been in Huban, Farhan more relaxed. Yet their stint in the capital had been before they'd gotten this close. Perhaps, hopefully, their newfound intimacy would continue once they were back in the palace, despite the additional pressure Farhan would be under.

He was needed back in Huban, and their schedule would have to be accelerated.

"The surgeon who was missing the day we arrived has left the islands to return to his home, and the hospital is short-staffed. I think they may have fired him for his unreliability. The director is requesting that I do some elective surgeries to allow them to catch up. They've already hired a replacement, but he won't be arriving for a while."

They'd spent the day traveling around the

largest of the southern islands, visiting a variety of rural clinics as well as the main hospital. Here, where there seemed to be a preponderance of women from mostly conservative families, the idea of a women's clinic was more popular. But even they agreed, barring that, an increase in female doctors might work just as well.

"Women understand women better," a councilwoman said to Sara. "It's more than just not wanting a strange man touching me. It's also trying to explain to a male doctor something he has only read about in books but has never experienced for himself or has any chance of experiencing."

It was enlightening to see the difference between the attitudes in the northern islands in comparison to those in the south. They were all a part of Kalyana, but although the country itself was small, there was a lot of diversity in the way people lived and thought.

When she mentioned that, Farhan said, "That's one of the facts the monarchy ignored here for a long time. Queen Nargis treated all her subjects as though they were homogeneous, and everyone suffered for it. My father has his faults, can be stubborn and old-fashioned, but both he and my grandfather at least acknowledged the necessity of understanding the people and their various needs."

"And you're working to expand that understanding." It gave her a little rush of emotion, but she tamped it down. "It bodes well for the country's future."

His expression was pensive, and he lifted her hand to kiss the inside of her wrist, making her shiver, before he replied.

"Honestly, I feel ill prepared to rule. While I don't regret my years away, sometimes I wonder if I shouldn't have ignored my father and stayed after Ali died. Even now, my father seems reluctant to instruct me in various ways. I'm constantly feeling as though I'm winging it."

Squeezing his fingers, she said, "I can't speak to your father's state of mind, but I have no doubt you'll be a wonderful king when the time comes. You're smart, compassionate, and thoughtful." She hesitated for a moment, then continued, "Perhaps you're better off forging your own path anyway, rather than following the one set by your father and grandfather.

After all, times have changed, and even the monarchy has to change with it."

He nodded, but didn't reply. The silence between them grew, but Farhan was slowly rubbing his palm up and down her arm now, and gooseflesh popped up across her back.

And when he said, "Ready for bed, beautiful?" she eagerly went with him.

How could he be so happy and in so much pain at the same time? Farhan wondered, as he watched Sara stoop down to speak to an elderly lady who couldn't get up.

They were in the village of Manan, the southernmost habitation on the southernmost island, on the final day of their tour. When Sara had heard that the oldest living inhabitant of Kalyana lived at a nursing home in the village, she'd insisted on going there to visit her. It was just another indication of Sara's heart, and Farhan really didn't need the reminder.

At all.

In truth, he resented how much joy he felt around her. Emotion wasn't a part of the plan, yet here he was, having the shell he'd so carefully built up around his heart cracked, with the danger of it falling away altogether, letting her in.

Now he felt the danger of the situation he'd created acutely.

It had seemed the perfect plan: a marriage of convenience with no chance of it lasting.

No chance of rejection.

But all that had changed. Sara had changed him, fundamentally, at a soul-deep level. She'd made him look at things differently, somehow calming the storm he'd felt himself to be in the center of. He could face the future with the kind of equanimity he'd never thought he'd achieve. Yet somehow he doubted it would be the same without her at his side.

This wasn't how it was supposed to be. He wasn't supposed to crave her—her attention, smiles, time, body—the way he did.

Every night he told himself it would be the last time he went to her, but the next he was pulled right back, following a golden bond he now felt tightening around his chest. The only good thing was that she clearly had no urge to stay in Kalyana, although her love for the country, and the people, was patently clear. She still spoke often about getting back to her family, who were still calling on her as though she was the only one who could solve all their problems. About opening a clinic in Northern Ontario. Calling Trinka to check on Coconut, the dog she wanted to take back with her.

The dog he'd secretly, stupidly, sent a plane for, so it would be waiting for her when she got back to the palace.

Wanting to please her, like a besotted fool.

They still had months to go on their agreement. Would this drive to have her keep growing, until he wanted nothing more than to make her stay? Everything inside him rebelled at the potential agony such a situation would engender, yet there was a part of him that already hated the notion of her leaving at all.

It was untenable, but he'd got himself into the situation, and couldn't see a way out.

Do you even want one?

Only pride stopped him from growling aloud at the thought, and it took all his concentration to adopt a neutral expression so no one would guess his inner turmoil.

Sara finished talking and laughing with the elderly lady, who was approximately one hundred and four, according to the records, and came back over to join him and the rest of the official party. Her face was glowing, the love and joy she imparted to everyone around her almost visible to the naked eye. His chest ached just from looking at her, seeing the luminous beauty on display for all to see.

One of the nursing home attendants came by to whisper to the director and, as Sara rejoined the group, the director said, "I know you're on a tight schedule, but there is another patient of ours who would like to see you. He once was an aide to the Governor, and says he met you many years ago, Your Highness. If you have a few moments, I know he would appreciate it very much."

"Of course," Farhan replied.

As they walked down a corridor toward the room, the director said, "Mr. Raj has no family coming to visit him, and although he's not bedridden he's had a gastric upset, and we've kept him quarantined. He's no longer contagious, just a bit weak, and we didn't know you were coming, or we would have got him up. It will be real treat for him."

She opened a door, and ushered them into the small, neat room, where the patient lay. While his body was clearly thin and frail, making hardly a bump beneath the sheets, his eyes were bright.

Then Mr. Raj looked at Sara, and his eyes filled with tears, which overflowed down his cheeks.

Sara was at his bedside in an instant, leaning down to take his outstretched hand, bending to hear what he whispered to her.

She jerked upright, her face pale, her gaze swinging to find Farhan, as he stood at the foot of the bed.

He didn't know what the old man had said to her but her expression had him stepping closer, reaching to pull her away, but she avoided his hand.

"I-it's okay," she stuttered, but she looked past him at the other people in the doorway, and he saw the confused, almost frantic gleam in her eyes. "C-could we have a few minutes alone with Mr. Raj, please?"

CHAPTER FIFTEEN

FARHAN DIDN'T NEED to ask why, just moved toward the door, shepherding everyone in the room out in front of him, making polite noises as he went. Curiosity overwhelmed him as he firmly shut the door and turned back to the bed.

Sara was still pale, looked as though she were about to cry too.

"T-Tell him what you said to me," she said, reaching out and pulling Farhan closer.

"You are my granddaughter." It wasn't a question but a firm, convincing statement. "When I saw you on TV, saw you had married Prince Farhan, I knew."

A rush of mixed emotions fired through Farhan's blood, and he had to tamp them down, keep his voice level, as he said, "Are you sure, Mr. Raj? Princess Sara was adopted as a baby. Her roots are uncertain."

The look the old man gave him was just shy of scathing.

"She is Prince Bhaskar's daughter, and child of my daughter, Yolande. I know this to be true."

As though her legs wouldn't keep her upright anymore, Sara sank down onto the edge of the bed. Farhan noticed she hadn't relinquished Mr. Raj's hand.

"How…? What…?" She cleared her throat, and tried again. "Why didn't you say anything when everyone was searching for Bhaskar?"

Mr. Raj shook his head, sorrow making his already wrinkled face even more lined.

"My Yolande was just fifteen when I took her to Huban, where I was stationed as part of my duties to the then Governor. I don't know how or when she met Bhaskar but, just after we returned to the south, she disappeared. No one was very interested in finding out what happened to her, not when just after that Prince Bhaskar disappeared as well, and I never thought the two things were in any way related."

"How did you find out that they were, sir?" Farhan's heart was pounding. The air in the room felt close, arid, and it took all of his control not to react to what he was hearing.

"Many years later, my daughter contacted me by letter. She told me she was living in Canada, in a place called Fort McMurray, and confessed to what she'd done. Bhaskar had convinced her to go away with him, had arranged it all through a friend in England. They were happy, she said, and I knew revealing their whereabouts might endanger Yolande.

"I didn't dare tell anyone what had happened. The Queen was almost crazed in her grief, and I, perhaps cravenly, wished most of all for my daughter's happiness. If Queen Nargis had found out what had really happened, I have no doubt she would have sent soldiers to bring them back, whether they willed it or not."

"Do...do you know what happened to them?"

Mr. Raj shifted fitfully, and Sara rose to help him lean forward, rearranging the pillows behind his back.

"Thank you," he murmured, his gaze never leaving her face.

"You're welcome," she said, but she didn't smile. Her face looked pinched, suddenly exhausted, and Farhan wanted to take her away, leave the rest of the story untold, but knew he couldn't.

No matter how painful the end might be.

"Yolande kept in contact with me after that. They had taken new names, of course, and settled in a place where there were no Kalyanese immigrants. She was lonely, and homesick, but the greatest unhappiness in her life was that she was unable to conceive. She was in her late forties when she finally told me she was expecting. I was worried, for her, for the baby, and I was right to worry."

His voice broke, and a tear trickled down his cheek.

"Yolande wrote to tell me Bhaskar had died unexpectedly and she had decided to arrange for her baby to be adopted should anything happen to her. I wrote to tell her she could arrange to send the child to me instead, but I never heard back from her, and my inquiries into her well-being were too late. I eventually found out she had died in childbirth, and no one would tell me where her baby had gone."

Farhan felt the silence like a weight. He had his hand on Sara's shoulder, felt her trembling. There was one way to make sure the story was true, but it was the effect hearing this all was having on Sara that concerned him the most.

He smoothed his hand down her back, and she leaned into the caress.

"Do you remember the names they used in Canada, sir?" Farhan asked.

"Of course. Brian and Yasmine Haskell. Do you want to see a picture of your mother?" The last addressed to Sara.

"Yes, please."

"There's a box in the wardrobe. Bring it to me."

"Stay," Farhan said. "I'll get it."

When he put the small cedar casket in the other man's hands, Farhan found himself under scrutiny.

"I did meet you, many years ago, Your Highness, when you were just a small child. I hope you don't mind my telling the nurses about it, so as to see my granddaughter."

"Of course not, sir."

That earned him a small smile, before Mr. Raj turned his attention to the box. The picture was almost at the very bottom, and when he held it out to Sara, Farhan's breath caught in his throat. The resemblance between mother and daughter was obvious, their smiles identical, although Sara had inherited much from her father too. He'd seen her staring at Bhaskar's portrait in the palace, her gaze pensive, perhaps searching for the connection she couldn't feel.

Sara took it almost reverently, stared at it for a long, silent time. Tears streamed down her cheeks, but she seemed unaware of them until Farhan shoved his handkerchief into her hand.

Seeing her like that almost undid him.

His heart ached, feeling her sorrow and overwhelming joy as if they were his own.

He'd never been an emotional person. He'd pushed emotions away until they were like background noise in his life, not things that drove or spurred him on. Now he felt he was all emotion, driven by the need to protect and keep her safe.

But this encounter with Mr. Raj had made an already complicated situation even more complex, and Farhan wasn't sure how to deal with the fallout.

Sara was wrung out.

They'd stayed with her grandfather for hours, listening to his stories of her mother as a child, reading the letters Yolande had sent her father. The last one had made her cry. Her mother's anguish at the loss of her husband had seemed to pour off the page.

She'd promised to come back and see her grandfather the following day, although they were supposed to go back to Huban that evening. Having just found him, she didn't want to simply disappear.

Farhan had questioned the nursing home staff about his condition. Anupam Raj was in fairly good health, although his stomach bug had laid him low for a little while. He was in the nursing home, they said, because he had no family still alive.

Her heart had ached when they'd said that, knowing the loneliness he'd experienced over the years while his daughter had been gone, hiding so as not to be torn away from the man she'd loved.

"Perhaps if my wife were alive, she would have realized what was happening between Yolande and Bhaskar, but she died when Yolande was just eleven, and I was raising her on my own. I was consumed by my work, trying to make sure I could give her a good life, send her to university, give her whatever she needed. I wasn't paying attention to the signs."

So much heartbreak in his life. Sara wanted to ensure his last years were happier.

But just finding him had changed everything.

She'd heard Farhan quietly ask her grandfather to hold onto the secret of her father's identity a while longer, and the old man's promise to do so. Now she had to try to figure out what that question meant, both for her and her future in Kalyana.

The agreement between herself and Farhan hadn't truly taken into consideration what would happen should someone come forward to name her the daughter of Bhaskar. He'd been so sure no one would that he'd said a year would be long enough for them to remain married. She'd been so eager for adventure she'd said yes, never contemplating how the journey would change her life.

How being Farhan's wife, his lover, would change everything.

More and more she felt the chains binding her to Kalyana tightening.

It all felt surreal. She'd thought the story of her birth would remain a mystery. Oh, she'd believed Farhan when he'd said Bhaskar was her father, had even looked at his portrait in the palace gallery, but she'd felt nothing. He'd been a handsome face on the wall. But seeing her mother's photograph, hearing their story had brought such a welter of emotions she wasn't sure how to deal with it.

Kalyana had truly changed her forever.

And now her time here, already limited, seemed set to be cut short.

How could she leave so soon, just when things between her and Farhan were so good? When her heart wasn't ready for the separation?

"Are you all right?"

They were in the back of the official vehicle that had driven them around all day. Outside the windows it was dark, shadows of trees flashing by against an only slightly less dark sky. They'd stayed way past when they were supposed to get back to the plane, and she suspected, while she'd been caught up in the moment, Farhan had made all the necessary arrangements for them to stay the night.

She appreciated it, but couldn't muster any energy to think about anything else but her grandfather's story and wondering what would happen next.

"I'm fine," she replied, but reached blindly

across the seat for his hand, desperately in need of human contact.

In need of him.

He took it, his thumb rubbing over her knuckles in gentle, soothing circles. And it did soothe her.

When had he become so important to her emotional well-being?

The question caused an icy shiver up her spine, and she pushed the thought away, too drained to deal with it just then.

"I have to return to Huban tomorrow morning."

"Yes," she replied. He had surgery scheduled for the afternoon. They were counting on him to help with the backlog. Was it terribly selfish to want him to stay, even knowing the hospital needed him?

"I'll send the plane back for you, unless you want to remain longer."

"No." She was in a fog but, even to her, her monosyllabic responses sounded rude. "No, I'll visit Grandfather in the morning and come back to Huban in the afternoon. That way I can get started making arrangements for him to come too." Having just found him, she wanted him close by.

"Leave that to me," he said, in his usual no-nonsense way. "I can handle it for you."

It made her, stupidly, want to cry again, but she quashed the urge. His poor handkerchief was already a damp, wrinkled mess from before, and she'd run out of tissues.

"I'm sorry," she said instead. "For disrupting everything."

"There's nothing to apologize for," he replied, squeezing her fingers. "You didn't plan any of this, neither was it of your making."

He was so understanding, her heart ached. Why did he have to be so perfect? She turned her hand to squeeze his fingers in return, thankful to have him on her side.

And later, when he came to her room as usual, he said, "I thought you could use some company. Not sex, just company."

That's when she knew there would never be another man for her. She was resigned to leaving, because she wanted all of Farhan, not just sexual attention, dribs and drabs of affection.

All of him; heart, body, and soul, if that were even possible. Just as she'd given him.

Nothing less would do for her.

And no other man would do either.

He held her, and she contemplated the lonely years ahead. Not unfulfilling, she decided, just not the home and family life she'd always thought she'd eventually have.

Not this feeling of safety she had lying in Farhan's arms.

Or the soul-shaking rush of emotion whenever they made love.

All the feelings of the day whirred together in her head, keeping her awake, restless.

So she rolled over, trapping him under her body.

"What is it, beautiful? Are you okay?"

She didn't want to talk. Instead, she wanted to somehow transcribe her inner emotions into the physical. Leaning down, she kissed him, taking the lead, their tongues tangling together deliciously.

He groaned, putting up no resistance, letting her love him as much as she wanted. As she slid down his body to kneel between his thighs, she could see his eyes gleaming in the weak moonlight coming through a crack in the drapes.

Over the last days she'd gotten bolder, but had never been this assertive.

"Lift," she said, tugging at the waistband of his silk pajama pants, and he did as bidden without a word.

But as she tugged them off, he said quietly, carefully, "We don't have to do this, beautiful."

She took his erection in her hand and said honestly, "I've never felt I *have* to do anything with or for you, Farhan. I want to. I need this tonight."

Taking him to the brink with her hands and mouth gave her such intense satisfaction it was as though he was touching her in return.

"Beautiful, please," he whispered, his body tense, bowing in ecstasy.

It was a plea, whether for her to stop or for the release building in him she didn't know. Giving him pleasure took her outside herself, to a place where all she thought about was him, all she felt was the love inside, now acknowledged, growing stronger each minute.

When he lunged up to take her by the shoulders and drag her body up over his, she laughed, making him growl in response.

"Are you trying to make me go insane?" he asked against her lips.

"Maybe I am," she replied, sliding back, taking him deep in one quick motion, her heart singing when she heard his rushed exhalation, blown out as though forced from his lungs.

Then she slowed, suddenly not wanting to hurry, taking her time as she rose and fell, savoring each heart-stopping sensation, feeling his body coiling and moving beneath hers. The tension built within, but she was no longer afraid of it, just let it take her to where that golden moment of bliss waited.

Farhan's hands on her breasts, her belly, pushed her arousal even higher, until she couldn't maintain her leisurely pace anymore.

"Yes. Oh, yes," she whimpered, as Farhan reached between them, stimulating her with exquisite finesse, taking her to the edge.

Tonight he lost control first, and she reveled in hearing his orgasm, knowing she'd taken him there. Then the pressure of his thumb increased, and she was flying too.

As, still draped across his body, she came

down from her high, two thoughts struck her in quick succession.

She'd never been more confused.

And they'd forgotten to use a condom.

CHAPTER SIXTEEN

SARA HADN'T EXPECTED Farhan to be at the airport when she arrived back in Huban, and he wasn't. He'd slipped out of bed while she was still asleep to go to the airport, and waking up without him beside her had left her feeling lonely and afraid.

She'd hoped to talk to him about what they were going to do next. Yet, in the light of day, her fears regarding Farhan's reaction had waned, seemed unwarranted. Yes, the revelations of the day before had come as a shock, but did they truly sound the death knell to their marriage? Did they have to?

Even the thought of her grandfather's story getting out didn't frighten her the way it perhaps should. Yes, she was the only one in love, but they'd grown so close, was it unreasonable to hope one day he might love her in return?

He himself had said arranged marriages were traditional in his family, and that was what they had. Couldn't they, somehow, make it work? Even his assertion that he didn't want children didn't deter her from her optimism. If, in time, he changed his mind, or even if he never did, Sara knew Farhan was the one man for her. The night before she had been resigned to leaving him. Today all she wanted was to stay, forever.

If that made her contrary, so be it.

"Crown Prince Farhan is still in theatre, Your Highness," Kavan said, as he ushered her to the black SUV he usually drove. "He's asked me to take you back to the palace, and inform you he might not be home in time for dinner."

"Thank you, Kavan," she said, wondering why Farhan hadn't texted as much.

"And King Uttam has requested you meet with him at four o'clock, in his office."

That was new, and she doubted Farhan knew about it, since he *definitely* would have texted.

"I'll be there," she told Kavan, who informed her he would advise the King's aide-de-camp Joseph Malliot.

No doubt King Uttam wanted to discuss her finding her grandfather, and she only just stopped herself from nibbling on the side of her fingernail, as she wondered what he would have to say.

It was obvious that while Anupam Raj had been a respectable man, he was definitely not royalty. Perhaps Uttam would resent mingling her blood with the royal line, now that they knew for sure who her mother was.

When she got back to the palace and was greeted by a wriggling ball of brown fur, she knew her hopes for a future with Farhan weren't misplaced. For him to have had Coconut brought to Huban for her spoke volumes about his character and, she thought, how much he cared about her happiness.

Later that afternoon, when Joseph ushered her into King Uttam's office, she found it empty, a red macaw in a cage the only occupant. As the bird seemed to try to attract her attention, Sara noticed the French doors opening into a private garden were ajar, and she walked over to look through them.

There was her father-in-law, seated on a bench, smoking a thin cigar. He saw her in the doorway, and waved her over.

"Please don't lecture me," he said, his stern lips twitching at the corners. "I used to smoke these things all day, every day, but have cut down to one a week."

He patted the bench beside him, and Sara dutifully sat, turning slightly so she was facing him.

"With that amount of restraint, couldn't you find it in yourself to quit entirely?" she asked, although she wanted to smile, seeing Uttam so relaxed.

"I didn't want to," he replied, then took a puff. "Life is short and should, whenever possible, be enjoyed. I know my family worries about me after my health scare, but carrying the burden of rule makes me testy. I think I deserve a little treat every now and then."

"Well, kudos to you for cutting back that much and not just starting up again. Most people couldn't do it."

His chin tipped up and, in that instant, Sara saw once more the resemblance between father and son.

That definitely was where Farhan got his arrogant look but, with Farhan anyway, she knew it wasn't really arrogance that made him look down that nose of his. He did it when he was in any way unsure, or perhaps embarrassed, and trying to hide it.

"A royal must have a strong will, and do what is right, no matter how difficult that may be. Farhan has learned this, as I think you have already also."

He sounded so snooty Sara was at first taken aback and then had to suppress a giggle. Luckily, the King was studying the end of his cigar, not looking at her, and didn't notice.

Uttam fussed with his cigar for a moment, relighting it when it looked as though it might have gone out, and then, wreathed in fragrant smoke, said, "I heard about your discovery while in the south."

"Yes," she replied cautiously.

"I remember Anupam Raj well. He was still in government service when we came here in the nineteen-sixties. A respectable man, who must have mourned as much for his daughter as Queen Nargis did when Bhaskar disappeared."

"Yes," she said again, not knowing exactly where the conversation was going.

"Farhan has informed me that Anupam will be coming to live here, in the palace, to be close to you, as his last living relative."

That she hadn't known. She'd thought perhaps Farhan would find a nearby nursing home, where she could go and visit him whenever she wanted, but her heart lifted to know he'd be even closer.

"I would appreciate you allowing that, Your Majesty," she said, trying to be as formal as she could, hoping Uttam wasn't going to refuse.

He gave her a stern, sideways glance.

"Of course I will allow it. Neither you nor he had anything to do with your parents' decisions, and shouldn't suffer for them."

"Thank you."

He inclined his head slightly, before continuing, "Your parents, your father in particular, did a great wrong to my family, but now you have the chance to make it right."

A bubble of resentment rose in Sara, and she was forced to bite the inside of her lip not to answer back. He'd just said neither her grandfather nor she were responsible for what had happened, but now it was on her shoulders to fix it? How unfair could you be?

Luckily, before she lost control and responded, Uttam went on.

"The important thing now is that you give

me a grandchild. Only then will it be safe to tell the people who you truly are, and they will know Bhaskar's line continues, to one day rule the country again."

Again she had to bite back a retort, annoyed by the arrogant way he demanded she bear a child, as though it were no more than telling her to cross the grass and pick him a flower. Did he not know how Farhan felt about having children? The urge to tell him, to lay it at his feet in spite, was almost overpowering.

Unaware of her resentful thoughts, Uttam said, "I was not always the best of fathers. Believe me, I'm fully aware of that fact, and now, in my old age, regret time not spent with my sons."

He gazed out over the gardens, his face as stern as ever, but Sara heard the undertone of sorrow in his voice and her anger faded, as he continued, "You know the saying? *There are three things in life you cannot recover: the word after it is spoken, the moment after it is missed, and the time after it is gone.* It is indeed true."

In that moment Uttam wasn't a king, just a

man searching his soul for answers, haunted by the past and all its attendant pain.

"Yes," she replied. "It's very true. But there are still time and moments to come, words yet to be spoken."

In the silence that fell between them, broken only by birdsong, her own ghosts stirred, and she wondered if Uttam's did too.

The King seemed to shake off his momentary melancholy, reaching over to pat her hand.

"My consolation is I know Farhan will do much better as a father, and as a king."

Cautious, but resolved, she replied, "Perhaps, Your Majesty, those are words you might say to him. Ones neither of you would regret?"

He turned his stern gaze on her and she saw the pain in his eyes fade to something softer, more contemplative.

"Perhaps you're right, Sara, although old habits die hard."

"That's true too, sir, but sometimes we have to forge new ones, for the benefit of ourselves and others."

Uttam smiled, and Sara was amazed. Farhan

really was the spitting image of his father, right down to the gorgeous smile.

And how stingy they were with them.

"My son is lucky to have you at his side. You'll make a good queen one day, and bear me strong grandchildren. That's imperative. With my health not being the best, I'd like to see my future heir before I die."

Taking that as dismissal, she rose. "I hope that day is a long way away, sir."

To her surprise, Uttam rose too, and bent to kiss her on one cheek then the other.

"No doubt Farhan feels the same way too," he said, in a jovial manner, turning her toward the French doors inside. "All he really wants to do is be a doctor. I hoped to let him do it as long as possible, away from the royal responsibilities we all find so onerous, but my health cut his time away short. He has much to learn, though, so it's a good thing he came back when he did, and didn't wait until he had to take the throne himself."

Did Farhan know that was why his father had let him return to Australia? Somehow she doubted it. When Farhan spoke about his father telling him to go back after Ali died, she'd heard deep pain in his voice, a diminishing of the proud self-confidence she associated with him. Hopefully, hearing the real reason, and that his father was truly proud of him, would take away the last vestiges of hurt and constraint between father and son, or at least help to bring them a little closer.

Although, dealing with two such proud men, it might not.

Uttam strode around his desk and pulled out his chair as Sara reached for the office door handle, and she had her back to the King when he said, "I was happy to hear that you refused to consider my offer of financial compensation for giving Farhan an heir. It showed good character."

She froze, not sure she'd heard the King correctly, and said without turning around, "Excuse me, sir?"

Uttam went on, as if he hadn't heard her question, "I would have been willing to pay twice as much to secure peace in our country, but it is better that you do it out of duty rather than financial gain."

"Yes, sir," she murmured, suddenly cold inside.

It reminded her forcefully of why she was there, how Farhan had viewed her when he'd found out about her. How he'd been sure that giving her money would be the way to get her to agree to his deal. He hadn't known the money, while welcome, had been only a small part of the reason she'd said yes.

But maybe he had, when he'd said she should consider the lump sum her inheritance from Bhaskar. In doing that, he'd made her feel she wasn't selling herself to him but, in fact, would be entering into a mutually beneficial arrangement.

Besides, it was different now, wasn't it? Now that he knew her? Surely he could see the money wasn't that important to her? Sure, she'd paid off her student loan, arranged to buy her parents a house and cover the upkeep, but the only other expense she'd taken on had been paying for Nonni's nurse.

Yet as she made her way back to their apartments, telling herself Farhan must, by now, know her better than to think she was in it only for the money didn't really help. Uttam's final words had dimmed the bright flame of confidence only just lit that morning.

* * *

Farhan didn't get back to the palace until late that evening, but he found Sara waiting up for him. He'd texted earlier to say there was a patient he wanted to monitor a bit longer than usual, a woman who'd undergone a bilateral salpingectomy, but who also had a history of dangerously high blood pressure that didn't respond as expected to medication.

"You didn't have to wait up for me," he said, holding himself in tight control, refusing to give in to the temptation to go over and kiss her, the way he'd gotten into the habit of doing.

"I couldn't sleep anyway," she replied. "Too much excitement over the last couple of days, perhaps. And I wanted to talk to you."

She looked tousled, as though she'd lain down and got back up again, cozy in her plush robe, her legs tucked up under her, Coconut lying across her lap. Farhan's heart contracted, his stomach ached, and he knew his decision to let her go was the right one.

He'd always planned to. Even on the days when he'd seemed to think almost exclusively about her, he'd reminded himself she wasn't meant to stay. That she'd be leaving sooner rather than later.

Meeting Mr. Raj had simply accelerated the timeline. If she didn't leave soon, his father would want to tell the people about her origins, and then she'd be trapped. Or, at least, her leaving would be more difficult.

He hadn't planned to discuss it with her tonight, had convinced himself to put it off for a while longer, but now, seeing her, wanting her so badly, he knew it had to be soon.

As Farhan lowered himself into an easy chair, he asked, "Is something wrong?"

She shook her head.

"On the contrary. I wanted to thank you for Coconut, and for arranging for my grandfather to come and live at the palace."

"How did you hear about that?"

"It was your father who told me."

Surprised at the mention of Uttam, he frowned. "You went to see my father?"

"He invited me and, of course, I went. It was an interesting talk. Do you know he let you stay in Australia as long as he did because he knew all you wanted was to practice medicine? He knew once you came home, you'd get bogged down by your position as Crown Prince and all the royal duties you'd have to take on."

Now it was shock making his eyebrows rise, even as he struggled to maintain a neutral expression. How was she able to get his father, who never spoke of personal matters, to open up that way?

Then her words struck home, and he only just stopped himself from gasping as his breath caught in his throat. Could that really be the truth? It was almost unfathomable, unbelievable. Yet he knew his father never said anything he didn't mean, so...

Desperate to change the subject, unable to discuss it further, he pulled himself together and said, "But I'm sure he didn't summon you to talk about my time in Australia. What else did he have to say?"

"He wanted to make it plain he expected me to quickly produce an heir, so he could tell the people about who my father was."

Another blow to his composure, which was becoming increasingly difficult to hold onto. Rising restlessly, he strode across to the sideboard and poured himself a finger of Scotch.

Now, more than ever, he was aware of the need to let Sara go, before it was too late.

If it wasn't already.

Memories of the night before rose, unbidden, into his head. The rush of emotion when she'd turned to him, wanting his comfort; the immediate arousal, as she'd made her delicious intentions known. Her shadowy form above him, the sensation of being enveloped by her sweet, hot body.

His desire for her didn't rise slowly, like smoke, to fill him. It was, instead, as though a hidden volcano released all its lava at once to rush through veins and sinews, burning all thoughts but those of her from his head.

He couldn't be trusted to do the right thing, to stay away, to keep his distance. It all had to end.

Taking a swallow of Scotch, he found the strength to turn and face her before he said, "Well, if my father is getting involved, perhaps it's time to put an end to this game, and have you return home."

CHAPTER SEVENTEEN

SHOCK TURNED SARA'S insides to ice, and all she could do was stare at his stoic, noncommittal expression in disbelief. The flame of hope, kindled by the connection she felt to him, his actions toward her, waned to a flicker in the face of his words. "What?"

"I believe it's the logical thing to do at this juncture. What started as a simple business contract has become something far more complicated, and I think it should end, before we find ourselves in a situation neither of us wants."

The little flicker of hope died, leaving Sara cold. So cold she had to clench her teeth to make sure they didn't chatter.

When she didn't reply, Farhan continued, in the same matter-of-fact voice as before, "It's not as though we ever intended our arrangement to last very long. It's just been cut shorter by circumstances, and I'll consider your side of the agreement fulfilled."

Rising, she set Coco on the floor and turned her back on Farhan. The little dog whined, coming to lean on her leg, as Sara clenched her fingers together across her stomach. The brief respite from being under Farhan's unemotional gaze steadied her, allowed her to control the thoughts whirring in her brain.

When she unclasped her fingers before turning to face him, the blood rushing into her abused digits gave her additional strength.

"And what if our slip last night has unwanted consequences?"

An unreadable expression flashed across his face and then, just as swiftly, was gone, leaving Sara to wonder if it had even really existed.

"We'll wait to make a final decision until we know whether that is the case or not."

Carefully bracing herself so her trembling legs wouldn't betray her, Sara tried to maintain an air of cool reasonableness, even though inside she was dying slowly, bit by bit.

Pride wouldn't let her argue. Especially not in the face of his emotionless, arrogant stance.

Yet hadn't she already discovered he was often at his most emotional, his most vulnerable when he cloaked himself in haughtiness?

When his chin tipped up and he looked down his nose?

She glanced at his hands, saw the white knuckles where he gripped the rock crystal glass, the bulge of the other hand fisted in his pocket.

What was he really feeling? Worried she'd make a scene? Upset his plan had fallen apart? Or was there something else?

There was no way for her to know, so all she said was, "If that's what you want."

Again there was a flash of emotion, in his eyes this time. Then he looked down at his glass as it rose once more to his lips, and it was lost to her.

There was nothing more to say, was there?

She'd turned toward her bedroom, Coco at her heels, when he said, "In case you're wondering, I'll compensate you as though you were here for the year."

Something snapped inside her. Perhaps it had always been there, this resentment, needing only this final nudge to be released.

Did no one want her just for herself? For the person she was inside?

The King saw her as a means to reclaiming his family honor and giving Kalyana an heir.

Her sisters saw her as a means for them to keep drifting through life.

Even her parents, who she knew loved her, saw her as an emotional, and sometimes financial, prop.

And now Farhan couldn't see past her usefulness to the woman who loved him, would do anything for him, if he could only love her in return. Had the nerve to speak to her as though she were nothing but a hireling.

She deserved better than that, from all of them, and as rage built inside her, determination to get her due rose with it.

Spinning around, she glared at him.

"Don't you dare speak to me about money right now. It's bad enough knowing your father wanted to pay me to carry your baby, without you getting into the act. If you want the damn money back, I'll work the rest of my life to make sure you get it, even what you deemed my 'inheritance.' I don't need anything from you. Ever again."

He paled, took a step toward her, but she backed away from his outstretched hand. Her chest was tight with anger, pain like a band around her heart.

"No, I don't want it back, Sara. I'll not accept it. Please, hear me out—"

"No! I could forgive your father for thinking throwing money at me would be effective before he met me, but I'll never forgive you for degrading my time here, as though money was all I was in it for. I guess it just goes to show I'm better off leaving, since you clearly don't know me at all."

She heard him call her name as she spun around, but ignored him, controlling her steps so as not to run, keeping her head straight, so he couldn't see her tears.

The best days of her life had just turned into the worst, and there wasn't anything she could do about it.

Yet, despite her pain and anger, Sara sat on the edge of her bed a week after the confrontation with Farhan and cried, as she realized her period had come.

There would be no baby from her last night of bliss with him.

In the days leading up to this moment, she'd come to the realization that if she were pregnant, staying in Kalyana would be the right thing to do. She'd seen carrying his child as an out, of sorts; a way to do what she really wanted to do anyway, but without taking responsibility for the decision.

A cowardly way of dealing with the problem, which had now been taken away.

And she'd spent no time planning for her departure, ignoring the coming eventuality as though to do so would make it go away. Now she had to consider how to get not only herself but her grandfather and Coconut back to Canada too.

She'd have to ask Farhan, but he'd retreated into the stern, stoic man she'd first met; unfailingly polite but cool and distant, and Sara tried to be the same.

It was the hardest, most heartbreaking situation she'd ever been in, but she knew leaving was really for the best.

She didn't want Farhan's friendship, his companionship, or protection alone. She wanted his love as well. And nothing less would do.

Throwing herself into work at the hospital was an outlet for the nervous energy inside, and it became lifesaving, allowing her to focus on something other than her dumpster fire of a life.

Just went to prove that being royalty, and rich, didn't make life all rosy.

Additional pressure from her sisters didn't help.

Mariah called to ask whether Sara was sending extra money home.

"It's the least you can do, to help Mom and Dad," she said.

But Sara wasn't falling for that. The time to stand firm with everyone in her life had come, finally.

"I've made arrangements to buy Mom and Dad a house, and I'll be taking care of the house expenses, but beyond that, I'm not taking responsibility for all of you anymore."

Even if it meant working herself to the bone to make sure they were secure, while also paying Farhan back. Despite his saying he wouldn't take her money, she was still determined to do it.

When Mariah spluttered and started trying to guilt Sara into more, she put her foot down.

"Listen," she told her sister. "You need to get your life together, and I'm willing to help you do it, but I'm not indiscriminately throwing money your way. You and Cyndi need to grow up and start taking responsibility for yourselves. You deserve more than you're allowing yourself to achieve."

That was the furthest she was willing to go, and she was drawing a line in the sand.

She couldn't bring herself to be as firm with her parents, but she'd noticed there were fewer calls and texts since Nonni had accepted the nurse and things had settled down for Aunt Jackie. Sara knew their dependence on her had been her own fault and she was resigned to continuing as she'd started, but maybe because of the distance they were finding their own way.

When she went back, it wouldn't be to London anyway. It was time to use her new-found assurance to advance in her career.

Now, drying her silly tears, she went to wash their tracks off her face, to make sure Farhan wouldn't know they had ever been there. Their breakfasts together were sporadic. She'd gotten into the habit of checking his schedule to get an idea of what time he'd be departing for the hospital in the morning. That way, sometimes she left earlier than he did, or vice versa, neither wanting to spend more time with the other than necessary. This morning, however, she planned to let him know there was no chance of them having conceived, glad it would mean her time with him, here, was up.

Staying in Kalyana was breaking her heart. It was as though love was all around her, yet just out of her reach. Her feelings for Farhan hadn't changed, even knowing Farhan didn't even care enough about her to truly get to know her, the way she felt she knew him.

Yet, did she really know him? She could have sworn there was more between them than just sex, or even friendship, but, then, what did she know? Thirty-one years old or not, in the end she'd turned out to be a silly virgin, falling for the first man who'd shown her any attention.

The thought was dismal, made her doubt some of the very attributes she prided herself on, like the ability to read people, to get a true sense of who they were. Damn him for not only breaking her heart but for making her doubt herself too.

Then she shook her head, knowing she'd done those things to herself, when she'd let herself fall in love with him.

Bracing herself, she left her room about the time she thought he'd be finishing breakfast.

Walking into the dining room, she saw him in his place at the table, reading a newspaper, and her heart stumbled over itself.

He was so handsome, even with slight bags under his eyes, and weary lines, which hadn't been there before, bracketing his mouth. He'd taken on a heavy surgical load, and the stress of doing that, along with his royal duties, showed.

Perhaps her news might lighten his load a little. It would be one less thing to worry about.

Taking a steadying breath, she walked to her chair. Hearing her footsteps, Farhan raised his head, and then stood.

"Good morning," he said, in his cool, measured way.

"Good morning," she replied, taking her seat. The attendant brought her tea, and she thanked him, then told him she would serve herself from the array of food on the sideboard. He melted away, knowing he would be summoned if needed thereafter.

"Will you still be going to the airport today?"

Farhan was looking back down at his newspaper as he asked, as though he couldn't even be bothered to meet her gaze while they spoke. It made her unbearably sad.

"Of course," she replied. "Is the flight still scheduled to arrive at ten?" Her grandfather was due to arrive from the south; arrangements Farhan had informed her of by text the day before. It was one more thing to worry about. How was she going to explain to Grandfather that, just as he'd come to live with her, she would be leaving?

"Yes."

"Good."

"Kavan will take you there. Will you be here, or at the hospital?"

The thought of mooching about the palace for three hours didn't appeal.

"At the hospital."

"I'll inform him."

"Thank you."

She turned her attention to her tea, depression settling like a cloak on her shoulders. Even in the beginning, when they'd hardly known each other, there'd been more ease between them. Now she felt as though Farhan had excised her cleanly, surgically, from his life in every important way there was.

Suddenly she was fiercely glad it would soon be over. To spend the rest of her life trapped in a marriage to a man she loved but who treated her with cool disdain would be intolerable.

Sara took a deep breath, knowing she should tell him but suddenly not wanting to, anxiety chewing at her insides at the thought of his no doubt cold reaction.

"I thought you should know, I'm not pregnant."

His head came up, and an expression she couldn't interpret crossed his face. His eyes flashed, as he stared at her, and then the stoic, controlled mask was firmly back in place.

"Thank you for telling me," was all he said, before looking back at the paper, leaving her breathless and bereft.

Farhan stared at the newspaper, the print dancing in front of his eyes, making no sense.

If he was honest, once Sara had entered the room he'd been unable to concentrate, reading the same lines over and over, the words having no meaning to his muddled brain.

Disappointment twisted in his belly, and he clenched one hand into a fist on his lap. She'd stated it so simply, without inflection, leaving him at a loss, unable to tell how she felt about the issue, left adrift on his own acidic sea of pain.

And for all his plans never to be a father, his surety he would turn out unfit for the task, regret ate at him now, and her words, when she'd accused him of never knowing her at all, still haunted him.

Locking it all away, the way he always did, had become almost impossible. She was on his mind almost every single waking moment. And now he faced the fact there was no reason for her to remain in Kalyana.

They should discuss her departure, all the plans that needed to be put in place for it to happen.

Instead he folded the paper and stood, leaving his half-eaten breakfast on the table.

"I'll let you know if there is any delay in Mr. Raj's flight."

By the time she said, "Thank you," he was already going out the door.

His cellphone rang as he was crossing the living room and, although he didn't feel like talking to anyone, he answered.

"Yes, Maazin?"

"I thought you should know, Cyclone Blandine has strengthened, and the meteorologists are beginning to think it will come this way."

Farhan stopped, forcing his full concentration on what his brother was saying. Kalyana was usually outside the path of storms in the Indian Ocean, but this one had formed further south than usual, and they'd been keeping an eye on it for the last couple of days.

"Do they have a prediction of when it might hit?"

"They're still not completely sure it will. There's some debate about whether wind shear will slow it down and eventually change the path, but I think we should continue making preparations."

"Yes," Farhan replied. They'd already put the emergency plan into action, but there was so much else that needed to be done. "By the time they know for sure whether the islands will get hit or not, it would be too late to get everything done otherwise."

"I'm putting together a further action plan right now, and I'll email it to you. Are you operating over the next few days, or will you be available to help?"

"All my scheduled surgeries are elective, so I'll cancel them. Better to not take the chance of having a patient with unexpected complications swell the ranks of the hospitalized. I'll get started on checking with the other hospitals, and making sure they're following emergency procedures."

"Good." Maazin was in full commander mode, his armed forces training kicking in. "Go over the emergency management plan, so you're fully briefed by the time you get the further action plan."

As he hung up the phone, Farhan was already thinking two steps ahead, although he was relatively sure Cyclone Blandine wouldn't come anywhere near them. Every few years there was a scare like this, but the prevailing winds usually kept the brunt of the storms offshore, with little or no landfall. And even when Kalyana was affected, it was just outer bands bringing rain and moderately high winds.

But it was better to take all the precautions and not need to than to be caught flat-footed.

"Farhan."

He turned to find Sara standing in the door-way from the dining room. Her face looked pale, and he could see how she gripped the doorjamb, as though to hold herself up.

He was about to ask if she was okay when she said, "Please make arrangements for me to leave, and for my grandfather to follow, if he wants to. As soon as possible."

Then, before he could reply, she walked away, her back straight, head high, leaving him suddenly unable to catch his breath.

CHAPTER EIGHTEEN

FARHAN STOOD IN the air traffic control tower at Huban International, and watched the smaller of the two royal jets taxi to the end of the runway. As it turned its nose into the wind, preparing for takeoff, his stomach twisted, his chest aching with a sensation he didn't want to name.

Sara was onboard, leaving. Going back to where she belonged, he told himself for the millionth time.

For expediency's sake, they'd told everyone she had a family emergency, which necessitated her returning to Canada.

"It'll be easier right now, what with all the preparations you're all doing in case the cyclone comes close," she said, her voice distant, as though she was already gone. "Once I'm settled, you can arrange for Grandfather and Coconut to join me."

Mr. Raj was the one person she'd been honest with. At least, Farhan assumed she'd been honest with her grandfather, since he'd agreed to go to Canada, but he hadn't been privy to the conversation. All he knew was Mr. Raj, while still as polite as before, had given him what could only be described as sorrowful looks the last time they'd met. But he hadn't expressed an opinion, or offered any advice, for which Farhan was immensely grateful.

His phone vibrated in his pocket, but Farhan ignored it, all his attention on the jet. He distantly heard the pilot ask for clearance, the familiar call sign making him clench his teeth with the effort not to tell the controller to deny them the right to take off.

Letting her go was the right thing to do. Why, then, did it feel so wrong?

Then, before it seemed he even had time to blink, the jet was airborne, banking, turning northwest.

He watched it until it was out of sight, frozen inside, thankfully numb.

As he finally forced his feet to move his phone buzzed again, and this time he answered.

"Yes, Maazin?"

"Father wants to see us both in his office. Have you left the airport yet?"

"On my way out now. I'll be there in twenty minutes."

"Did Sara get off okay?"

Just hearing her name threatened to break him, but he simply said, "Yes. See you at the palace."

They'd all been working flat out, trying to make sure everything in the emergency management plan was implemented, while Blandine waltzed back and forth in the Indian Ocean like a deadly flirt. Each time they thought they were clear, she sashayed south again, and they were back on alert. No doubt Uttam wanted an update on their preparedness, but Farhan wasn't in a position to add much to any discussions.

Oh, he'd done his part. Flying to Agung to take supplies and make sure the hospital there was following protocols, as well as overseeing the plan to evacuate people from some of the outlying clinics if necessary. But it had all been done on autopilot, his entire brain taken up with thoughts of Sara leaving.

Now, settling back in the car, he tried to get up to speed on what had been happening elsewhere, but couldn't concentrate on the emails

Maazin and others had sent. Instead, his mind insisted on taking him back through every moment of the time with Sara, from the jolt of attraction he'd felt that first night on her doorstep, to the moment she'd said goodbye.

"Be well, Farhan. Be happy." He'd wanted to answer, but his throat wouldn't work. It had been the expression in her eyes that had rendered him mute. One he recognized, but, even after all they'd shared, still didn't want to name.

He started as Kavan shut off the SUV, realizing they were already at the palace, although he couldn't remember a moment of the drive.

Get yourself together.

He needed to be on his toes to deal with his father right now.

The meeting went fairly quickly, with Maazin, thankfully, carrying most of the load, but when they rose at the end, Uttam said, "Farhan, a word."

Suppressing a sigh, he sank back down into the chair, was surprised when his father dismissed his aide, who usually stayed at his side in all meetings. Uttam fussed with some papers on his desk for a moment, leaving Farhan to wonder what, exactly, was going on.

When the door closed behind the others, his father finally turned his attention to Farhan.

"When is Sara coming back?"

He should have known it would be what was on his father's mind. It was the first time Farhan was glad his father's vision was so poor, so he couldn't see how the question caused his son to flinch.

"When she's settled things in Canada, sir."

"It was a bad time for her to leave, right in the middle of the preparations for the cyclone."

Farhan felt his hackles rise, but he kept his voice level, as he replied, "Sara did her part before she left. She ended up taking charge of the patient audit, and did a great job of it."

Uttam waved a hand. "I know." Then he shifted in his chair, as though uncomfortable, before continuing, "I would feel better knowing she was here to keep an eye on you, if the storm comes."

The words rocked Farhan back in his chair, literally. Then he understood. His father worried about losing another heir.

"Don't worry, sir. I'll be careful."

Uttam shook his head. "It doesn't matter if you are, Farhan. It won't stop me worrying about you, and your brother. Both of you have the drive to serve others, and would put yourselves in danger to do it, no matter the cost. It is a good attribute, and one of the many reasons I'm proud of you, so I suppose I shouldn't complain."

Too shocked to reply, Farhan stared across at his father, who had his chin tipped up and was looking down his nose, clearly uncomfortable with his unaccustomed display of emotion.

"Sara reminded me that just because I missed opportunities to speak or offer praise before, it doesn't mean new opportunities wouldn't arise. I felt this was one I shouldn't let pass. I grew up in a different era, Farhan. One where men didn't express how they felt, and were expected to keep everything locked inside. It became habitual for me, but I'm glad to know you don't have to follow suit. It will make you a better husband and father than I have been."

It was like looking in a mirror, but seeing his own reflection clearly for the first time, hearing a truth only his father, his mirror image, could tell.

Emotion wasn't the enemy. Locking it away was.

Sara too had tried to tell him that he didn't have to follow his father's lead, but he hadn't listened, too intent on holding onto past hurts, so as not to experience them again. And, in the process, he'd lost the best gift life could have given him.

Sara.

He rose, then hesitated. Found the words, then said them. "Thank you, Father. This means more to me than you could know."

Sara had the private lounge in Dubai International Airport to herself, and was glad of it. A steward fussed over her, until she told him, kindly but firmly, that she had all she needed.

What a lie.

What she needed was to get home to Canada, and get on with rebuilding her life. The delay—something about the plane needing a small repair—wasn't helping at all.

They were supposed to have flown straight on to London, where she would overnight, and then continue the journey the following day. The unexpected stop would be frustrating if she weren't so numb.

Even now, five hours into the trip, she couldn't believe she'd actually left Farhan, forever. Yet it was the right thing to do, for both of them. Hopefully one day he would wake up and realize he was so much more, so much better than he gave himself credit for. That he had more to offer than just being a surgeon, or a prince, or even a king, and it was within his capabilities to do all of them well, as well as being a wonderful husband and father.

As for her? She'd survive, but she was leaving love behind. Not because it was too painful, but because there would never be anyone like Farhan in her life again. He was one of a kind, and all she wanted. No one else would ever compare.

She closed her eyes, leaning her head back, ineffably weary, homesick for the place she'd just left her heart in.

"Is this seat taken?"

Eyes flying open, she spun in her seat, unable to believe what her ears were telling her.

But it was true. Farhan Alaoui, Crown Prince

of Kalyana, was lowering himself into the seat beside her.

"What are you doing here?"

He hesitated before answering, and then his chin tipped up, and he said, "I came to Dubai to tell my wife that I have been the biggest fool that ever was. That I love her with all my heart, and I'm hoping she'll come home with me, so I can prove to her, every day and every night, that I understand now."

"U-understand? Understand what, Farhan?"

"That running from my emotions, or locking them away, doesn't mean I don't have them. That fleeing from pain doesn't mean it won't catch up. That loving you isn't something to fear, but something to embrace, and be grateful and thankful for.

"And I understand, too, how I hurt you when I treated our relationship as though it were still a business deal, despite knowing it was far more. But I didn't want you to suffer, financially, for my own cowardice."

He reached for her hand, curved his fingers around hers, the touch like a balm to her battered, sorrowful soul, as he continued, "And I am grateful, and thankful for you, Sara. Perhaps you don't love me, but I know without a doubt you care about me, and if that's all you want to give, I will gladly take it."

Amazed, she shook her head.

"But you must know I love you, Farhan. That I didn't argue when you said I should leave because I couldn't settle for the crumbs of your affection, no matter how nicely you treated me or how good we were together in bed."

His fingers tightened on hers almost painfully, and his eyes flashed with that dark fire she loved so much. "Crumbs? You have my whole heart, beautiful. My soul. You're my everything. I should have told you how devastated I was when I heard you weren't pregnant; how much I'd hoped and prayed you were, so you would have to stay with me. If I have the honor of being father to your children, no one in the world would be happier than I."

Heart pounding, she stared at him, trying to decide whether he meant it or not.

But it was there, in his eyes, the tense set of his gorgeous mouth, even that arrogant tilt of his chin, letting her know it was real.

"Oh, Farhan."

And he must have heard the answer in her

voice, as he reached over the arms of their club chairs to pull her close.

"Tell me you love me again, beautiful," he whispered into her ear. "I need to hear it again."

So she told him, and, when pressed, promised to tell him every day for the rest of their lives.

For an instant time seemed to slow, allowing her to commit the moment to memory, like a snapshot. And in that single frame, safe once more in Farhan's arms, life truly was perfect.

"My Princess," he murmured. "My love, forever."

And Sara knew, like everything Farhan said, it was the truth.

The Surgeon Prince was hers, for always.

* * * * *